As Darcy put the pillow down,

she saw that there was something under it. A bear. A saucy brown plush bear with glittering black eyes and a red velvet ribbon—almost new. Darcy picked it up—and gasped.

The feeling that came from the bear was not of warmth or tenderness or love. It was black, cold, and evil. An overwhelming evil that seemed to rush at her in waves, pulling her under, like a heavy surf—

Chilled and frightened, Darcy closed her eyes and took a deep breath. Still holding onto the bear, she forced herself to think logically. I have to contact Vickie somehow. That's why I'm here. "Vickie," she whispered out loud, "where are you?"

The SUNSET ISLAND series
by Cherie Bennett

Sunset Island
Sunset Kiss
Sunset Dreams
Sunset Farewell
Sunset Reunion
Sunset Secrets
Sunset Heat
Sunset Promises
Sunset Scandal
Sunset Whispers
Sunset Paradise
Sunset Surf

The SUNSET AFTER DARK series
created by Cherie Bennett

Sunset After Dark
Sunset After Midnight
Sunset After Hours

Sunset
After Hours

CREATED BY
Cherie Bennett

BY SUSAN ALBERT

SPLASH™

A BERKLEY / SPLASH BOOK

SUNSET AFTER HOURS is an original publication of
The Berkley Publishing Group.
This work has never appeared before in book form.

SUNSET AFTER HOURS

A Berkley Book / published by arrangement with
General Licensing Company, Inc.

PRINTING HISTORY
Berkley edition / May 1993

A GLC BOOK

Splash is a registered trademark belonging to General
Licensing Company, Inc.

Sunset Island and *Sunset After Dark* are
trademarks belonging to General Licensing Company, Inc.

ISBN: 0-425-13666-3

A BERKLEY BOOK ® TM 757,375
Berkley Books are published by The Berkley Publishing Group,
200 Madison Avenue, New York, New York 10016.
The name "BERKLEY" and the "B" logo
are trademarks belonging to Berkley Publishing Corporation.

PRINTED IN THE UNITED STATES OF AMERICA

10 9 8 7 6 5 4 3 2

ONE

"How about if I add some more white to your hair?" Darcy Laken asked as she stood behind Molly Mason with a can of talcum powder and a brush. The two of them were in front of Darcy's mirror, getting ready for the horror costume party that Molly's parents gave every year in their Sunset Island mansion.

"*More* white?!" Molly squawked, pushing Darcy's hand away. "My hair already looks like a blizzard hit it. And you want to—"

Darcy grinned. "Hey, chill out, Mol. You're supposed to be Anthony Perkins's *mother,* right? The way I remember *Psycho,* she's got gray hair." Darcy stepped back and reached for a gray eye pencil. "A few more wrinkles wouldn't hurt either."

Molly tossed her head. "Yeah, but the way I remember *Psycho,* gray hair isn't all she's got. Mrs. Bates has a wheelchair—

1

like mine." She wheeled herself away from the mirror. "So let's just skip it with the gray hair, okay? And forget the wrinkles. I think I'll look enough like her with what I've already got. I don't want to look like Methusalah's grandmother."

Darcy shrugged. "You couldn't if you wanted to. You're too pretty. But have it your way."

Molly flashed her a quick, devil-may-care grin. "I usually do, don't I?" She snapped her fingers. "Come on, Elvira. Finish getting gorgeous. It's time to *party*."

Darcy returned Molly's grin and then turned to the mirror, looking herself over critically. Raven-black waist-length hair parted in the middle, high cheekbones, long dark lashes, and violet eyes. *Not bad,* she thought. Her slinky floor-length black dress was slit to her knees, and she'd made up her face with dead-white foundation and spots of rouge to look like Elvira, the late-night movie spook queen. Something was missing, though.

"Your lipstick," Molly said critically, breaking into Darcy's self-appraisal. "It's not dark enough." She fished through a drawer and found an old tube of lipstick. "Here. Try this."

The color was a dark plum, almost black

against Darcy's light skin. "Geez, Molly," Darcy objected, "this'll make me look like a ghoul."

"Yeah," Molly grinned. "That's the general idea, isn't it? From glamour girl to glamour ghoul with a few easy—"

"Cute," Darcy said archly. She opened the tube and outlined her lips. "What would I ever do without you, Mol?"

What would I do without Molly? It was a question that Darcy had asked herself ever since Mr. and Mrs. Mason had offered her a job as Molly's live-in companion. *Yeah, but being with Molly isn't just a job,* Darcy reminded herself. *It's a lot more than that. It's a way of making up, a little bit, for the accident.*

Not that the wreck had been her fault— another driver had slammed into Molly's car and put her in that wheelchair. *But I should have told her about my dream,* she told herself for the umpteenth time. *If I'd warned her, maybe it wouldn't have happened.*

The dream had been terrifyingly real, like the other premonitions Darcy had had since she was a child—she'd experience spine-tingling moments in which she saw an event exactly as it was going to happen in the future. ESP, people called it, having "second sight," being "psychic." *But it was so horrible,* she reminded herself. *I just couldn't believe it would come true. And I'd already screwed up that thing with Marianne Reed, telling her she had a brain tumor when she didn't. How could I trust myself to call Molly and say,* "Hey, Mol, I've had this weird dream about an accident and you'd better keep your butt out of cars for a while, okay?" That was one reason that it felt good to be able to take care of Molly. *I can't change what happened, but at least now I can help.*

Of course she gives me more than I give her, Darcy thought appreciatively, putting the finishing touches to her lipstick. *I always thought I had it rough, growing up on the wrong side of the tracks. I knew I had to be tough. But I didn't know what tough really was.*

Darcy turned away from the mirror. "Does this get it?" she asked, turning up her mouth in a vampirish smile.

"Gruesome," Molly said admiringly. "Mondo-bizarro. You are one sexy ghoul Darcy." She frowned at Darcy's nails. "But your nails are a total disaster. What have you been doing with them? Digging up corpses?"

Darcy laughed. "I just changed the oil in

4

the car this afternoon," she said. The Masons loaned Darcy their oldest car—they had four—to drive to the university in Portland where she was a freshman. Darcy had insisted on taking responsibility for the upkeep of the car. After all, it was the least she could do—the Masons paid her tuition and college expenses, in addition to a salary.

Molly shook her head. "I don't suppose it occurred to you to take the car to the Speedy-Lube."

"Are you kidding?" Darcy demanded indignantly. "Why should I shell out good money to some guy so he can do something I can do with my eyes closed?"

Changing the oil was something that Darcy's auto mechanic father had taught her to do while she was still in high school. *But it wasn't the only thing I learned from him,* she thought. *He taught me to take care of myself. To be strong and independent.* Of course, it didn't hurt that she was five-foot-nine in her bare feet, or that she had a diver's strength and suppleness, or that her two older brothers had pushed her to stand up and fight for her rights instead of knuckling under. She could be practically fearless, especially when her temper

5

was aroused, or when somebody she cared for was in danger.

"Just thought I'd mention it," Molly said with a grin. "Sit."

Darcy pulled back her hands, suspicious. "What are you going to do?"

"Fix you up with some fakes," Molly said. "I snitched them from my mother's prop kit. Now give me your hands," she commanded, "and stop acting like a jerk."

Darcy sat on the edge of her oak canopy bed as Molly started on her nails. She looked around at her room with the gleaming wood floor, the tapestry rug, the walk-in closet, its open, airy space. *It's almost as big as all the bedrooms in my parents' house put together,* she thought. Back home, she'd shared her dinky bedroom with her two sisters, Lilly and Patsi. Here, her mirrored bathroom was as large as that bedroom, with a sunken tub almost big enough for her to swim in. *And it's all mine!* she told herself. *All the years of not having enough—they're over.*

Darcy watched as Molly began to fit the fake nails. She still felt a little guilty for being so eager to get away from her family's shabby house. But she loved her parents and she knew they had done the best they could. When she was fourteen, her father had suffered a stroke and was on disability. Her mother, a waitress, struggled to make ends meet. *Now,* Darcy thought fiercely, *I can do something to make them proud of me. Now, I've got a chance to make it in the world, to make it big. And Darcy Laken isn't going to screw up.*

Molly applied the last dab of nail polish, sprayed on some dryer, and surveyed her work. "There," she said with satisfaction. "Sexy, huh?"

Darcy laughed. "Speaking of sexy, what time is Kenny coming?"

"Right when it starts, he said. He didn't want to miss any of the action. My parents do throw interesting parties!"

Kenny Streep was a guy Molly and Darcy had met at Foxfire Stables, his family's farm out on Shore Road, where he was the head instructor of a new paraplegic riding program. Kenny had been an avid rider until he fell and injured his back and became paralyzed from the waist down. But that didn't stop him from doing what he wanted to do. He'd been a real hero just after they'd met him, rescuing the horses— including Molly's beloved Ebony—from a burning barn.

Darcy recalled this incident and then

winced and pushed the memory out of her head. Thinking of the fire brought back a powerful memory of someone else. *Sweet, passionate, but mixed-up Tony,* Darcy thought sadly. It still hurt remembering the brief time they'd had together. She hoped that wherever he was now, things were better.

"How about Scott the Cop?" Molly asked. "He's coming, isn't he?"

Darcy shook off her memories. "You got it," she said. Scott Phillips, a Sunset Island policeman, was her boyfriend. Scott had been there for her when she needed him. She smiled, thinking of him—good-looking, honest, and nice. *Yes, I fell for Tony,* she thought, *but I came back to Scott. And he understood.*

"You know he wouldn't miss *this* party," Darcy said.

"You know, Darcy, Scott's a really great guy. I'm glad you're together," Molly said wistfully. "It makes me wish I could have something like that."

"My darling friend," Darcy replied breezily, "if I recall you have a certain Kenny Streep hot on your trail. And anyway, Scott hasn't even kissed me yet!"

Molly smiled. "Okay, okay, you win. I'll

skip the self-pity trip for the night. Are your new friends from school going to make it?"

"Yeah—Tia and Vickie. Vickie's just a little older than you, Mol. Tia said she skipped a grade in school, which would make her seventeen.

"Which class is Tia in with you? English?"

Darcy shook her head. "I met her at The Java a couple of days ago. She was reading this book on the history of witchcraft, which I thought was pretty weird. We got to talking about ESP and stuff. I like her—she's easy to talk to. And she seemed to really listen."

Molly raised both eyebrows. "Did you tell her? About you, I mean."

"A little," Darcy said. "She kept asking questions. She seemed kind of curious about my dreams." Darcy had learned by experience that most people were pretty skeptical about her psychic abilities, so she didn't advertise the fact that she had them. But Tia seemed so interested that it had been easy to tell her about the psychic flashes. Darcy had gotten the feeling that Tia was genuinely interested.

Downstairs, Darcy heard the echoing chunk-chunk of the door knocker, a sound like somebody pounding on a hollow coffin. "Hey, maybe that's the guys," she said.

"Well, what are we waiting for?" Molly said happily, wheeling for the door. "Let's cruise!"

Simon, the Masons's butler, stood by the open front door as they came out of the tiny elevator the Masons had installed after Molly's accident. "And just who," he was growling in his sinister, resonant voice to someone on the front porch, "are you?"

Molly wheeled herself off the elevator and looked through the front door. "Hey, Lurch," she said. "You know who that guy is. Freddy Krueger."

A figure stepped out of the shadows, wearing a Freddy Krueger mask, an old brown felt hat, a red-and-khaki striped sweater, and black pants. His fingers ended in dangerous-looking three-inch razors.

"Evenin', Lurch," "Freddy" growled.

"Indeed it is a good evening," Simon said. "Mr. Krueger, do come in." Simon's craggy face cracked into a grin, and he straightened his hunched shoulders in his rusty black tux. Lurch—the Addams Family butler—was Simon's hero, and he loved it when people called him that. Simon had met the Masons when he was playing a walk-on part as a vampire in one of their movies. Nearly six-and-a-half-feet tall, with eyes like black coals sunk into his head, Simon did a terrific vampire act.

Darcy stepped past Simon. "Is that you, Scott?" If he hadn't told her what his costume was going to be, she'd never have guessed.

Scott's hazel eyes peered at her from the mask. "Yeah, it's me," he growled in Freddy Krueger's voice. "I'm lookin' for Elm Street. And who are you?"

"Elvira, my dear!" Gomez, Molly's father, stepped out of the shadows. "And Freddy Krueger! How charming!" Gomez was wearing his normal day-time garb, which on anyone else would have seemed like a costume: a crimson satin smoking jacket with quilted lapels, black velvet trousers, and red velvet slippers. Behind him was Molly's mother, Caroline, her dark eyes heavily made up. She was wearing a low-cut dress with tight sleeves that came to a point over her wrists. The dress was white—or at least, it had been white. Now it was stained with what looked like blood, seeping from a hideous open gash on Caroline's shoulder. Her face and her long black hair were also streaked and clotted

11

with blood, and in her hand she carried a Spanish dagger, with a blood-stained blade.

"Looking good, Mom," Molly said cheerfully.

"Thank you, dear," Caroline said. She looked down at the dagger. "I'm not sure I want to carry this thing all evening, though. Why don't I just—" With a swift thrust, she jabbed it into the gash on her shoulder, where it stuck, quivering.

Scott pulled in his breath, startled. Even Darcy blinked. Then she laughed. The Masons were among the best B-grade horror-film writers in the business, and they lived in a world of their creations surrounded by the props and gimmicks from their old movies. They even used a hearse as one of the family cars.

The doorbell sounded—or rather, it shrieked as it was rigged to do, and Simon opened the door. Somebody in a wheelchair wheeled himself into the hall.

"Kenny?" Molly asked doubtfully. "Is that you?"

Darcy wasn't sure, either. The wheelchair was the only thing she recognized. In it hunched a tall, black-cloaked figure—headless. On its lap was an extraordinarily lifelike man's head, eyes wide open, staring, its tongue grotesquely lolling.

"The Headless Horseman!" Caroline cried, clapping her hands. "How marvelously ingenious, Kenneth!"

"Thank you," came a muffled voice from somewhere inside the cloak, and Darcy saw one eye peering out.

"Come out and join the party, Kenny," Darcy said, and Kenny's head popped out of the cloak.

"Whew," he said, running a hand through his russet hair, his hazel eyes twinkling appreciatively at Molly. His face was lean and handsome. "It's hot in there."

Darcy heard voices out front, and other guests began to arrive, some from Sunset Island and Portland, others were show-business friends of the Masons from as far away as New York. Darcy had to laugh when she watched them come in. Many had been in the Masons's house before and knew what to expect, but others were stunned into silence when they walked into a scene right out of a horror movie— the Masons's was an ancient, forbidding house with black shutters and a black front door that was ten feet high and had a door knocker in the shape of a skull. Inside was a formal hallway with black marble floors, skull-printed wallpaper, silky cobwebs draped from the shadowy ceiling, and a skeleton hanging from a noose in one dark corner. And of course there was Simon, the quintessence of ominousness, Caroline oozing blood, and Gomez happily oblivious to the strangeness of it all.

The house was full of costumed guests by the time Tia and Vickie arrived. Tia was wearing a King Kong costume, a gorilla suit with a massive rubber mask. And Vickie, a delicate, almost-beautiful blue-eyed blonde was dressed as King Kong's girlfriend. She was barefoot, in a shredded white dress, and her hair hung loose over bare shoulders. The costume gave her the look of a frightened child.

"Perfect outfits," Darcy said, as King Kong did a shuffling dance, beating on his chest. "Where'd you get that fabulous mask?"

"From Lucy in Disguise with Diamonds," Tia said, her voice muffled by the mask. "Across the street from The Java. It just opened last week." She opened her mouth and gave a loud roar.

Vickie smiled. "I volunteered to be Kong," she said, "but Tia wouldn't let me."

"I've always had this secret yearning to

be a gorilla," Tia said, letting out another roar. "Anyway, you can imagine Vickie trying to roar? She'd sound like a mouse."

Darcy laughed and introduced the girls to Molly, Scott, and Kenny. Tia pulled off her King Kong mask, shook out her heavy red-brown hair, and looked around. "Wow, what a party," she said, taking in the Phantom of the Opera, Dr. Jekyll and Mr. Hyde, a hunched-over gnome, and Riff-Raff and Meatloaf from "The Rocky Horror Picture Show," all gathered around the food table. The centerpiece on the table was a large cake made in the shape of the Mason mansion, with owls and bats perched on the roof.

"God," Vickie said, looking around, "I can't believe this place." She shuddered as she saw the skeleton fastened high on the wall.

Tia turned to Molly. "Don't tell me you actually live in this house."

Molly nodded gravely. "I'm forced to. Every time I try to escape, they lock me in again." She gave a heavy sigh. "Last time, Simon swallowed the key so I couldn't find it."

"Really?" Vickie squeaked, horrified. "But they have to let you out sometime, don't they? When they do, can't you make a break for it?"

"I did—once," Molly replied darkly. "How do you think I ended up in this?" She slapped the arm of her wheelchair. "I almost escaped, but almost wasn't good enough."

"Oh, how awful!" Vickie cried.

"Yeah, isn't it?" Darcy asked, straight-faced. "But you should see what comes later. At five minutes to midnight, Simon drags her upstairs and chains her to her bed." She lowered her voice eerily. "That's when she turns into something that isn't quite human, you see."

Molly raised both arms up, fingers like claws. "Aargh!" she growled ferociously, while Tia giggled and Kenny and Scott laughed.

Vickie finally caught on. She managed a weak smile, but Darcy noticed her looking nervously over her shoulder, as if she were waiting for Simon to come with Molly's chain.

Kenny turned to Molly. "Hey, Mrs. Bates," he said, "how about if we eat before those vampires disappear with the food?"

"Okay," Molly said with a laugh. "Come

on, Vickie. Stick with us and you'll be all right."

When they'd filled their plates, they wandered around for a little while, looking at the costumes and catching snatches of conversations—gossip about horror movies, ghost stories, and interesting tidbits about the movie industry. After they'd all eaten, Scott and Kevin disappeared in the direction of the pool table. The girls made their way to the family room, where some of the guests were watching an old horror movie on video—one of the Masons's movies, of course.

One end of the room was set up like a fortune-telling booth, with an Ouija table—a round table with letters of the alphabet painted on it. There were sheets draped from the ceiling, and eerily flickering candles. The girls wandered over to watch a woman dressed like the Wicked Witch in *The Wizard of Oz* and a man dressed like Leatherface in *The Texas Chainsaw Massacre,* sitting at the Ouija table.

"Ouija won't give me any messages tonight," the Witch pouted and got up. "It won't talk to me."

"That's because you're not tuned in to the cosmos," Leatherface replied. "You

have to be open. You have to be receptive."
He bent over to pick up his chain saw. "You
have to be willing to let it happen." He
yanked on the starter rope and the chain
saw roared to life. The Witch screamed and
ran away. Leatherface threw his head
back, laughing. "It doesn't have a blade on
it," he said to Darcy and Molly, "but it
spooks 'em every time." He turned off his
chain saw and walked away, still laughing.

Molly wheeled her chair to the table.
"Why don't we try a little Ouija," she
suggested. "Maybe the cosmos will talk to
us."

"What is it?" Vickie asked, leaning over
the table.

"It's a fortune-telling game," Molly replied. "It's kind of silly, but it's fun. Come
on, Darcy, let's try it."

"I don't think so," Darcy said. Her fingers were tingling strangely, and she felt
and odd wariness, like a cold knot, pulling
her stomach tight. *If I didn't know better,
I'd almost think I was afraid of it,* she
thought, and then laughed to herself.
Afraid? No way!

"It isn't a parlor game," Tia told Vickie.
She parked her King Kong head on the
floor beside the table. "The Ouija board
receives messages from the spirit world.

You put your fingers on the pointer"—she pointed to a triangular piece of plastic with casters under the corners—"and it moves around the board and spells things out."

Molly gave a laugh. "Hey, you sound like you really believe this stuff."

"I do," Tia said, her green eyes serious. "But it doesn't work for everybody." She glanced quickly at Darcy. "Only for people who've got the gift."

Darcy frowned. The candles flickered eerily, casting shadows over the board. *Why do I feel so weird?* she wondered nervously. *The Ouija board is just a stupid game!* Still, the eerie feeling persisted.

"Hey, no offense, Tia, but this Ouija stuff is not my idea of a good time," Darcy said lightly. "Why don't we go try to convince Gomez and Caroline to do their act before dessert?" Gomez had promised to saw Caroline in half sometime during the evening.

"I think you're more interested than you're letting on," Tia told Darcy, studying her intently.

"Well, you think wrong," Darcy replied.

"I'm interested!" Vickie piped up. She sat down at the table eagerly. "Come on, Molly. Try it with me. My psychology professor is always talking about ESP—

you know—extrasensory perception." She smiled shyly. "In fact, he says I've got it. He's been testing me. Maybe that'll allow us to communicate with the spirit world."

"Okay," Molly said, shrugging at Darcy good-naturedly. "Let's see who's sitting at the Great Switchboard in the sky." She wheeled closer to the table and rested her fingers on one side of the pointer. Vickie put hers on the other, and they waited. Vickie's fingers trembled a little, but the pointer didn't budge.

"Nothing's happening," Vickie said, sounding disappointed.

"Maybe the operator's on coffee-break," Darcy said dryly.

"The spirit world does not appreciate your sense of humor," Vickie warned.

Sure, Darcy thought, rolling her eyes. *What did the spirits do—phone in their disapproval?*

They waited another minute or two. "Well, so much for spirit messages," Molly sighed. "It's not working." She shoved the pointer toward Tia. "Here, you and Vickie try it."

"I keep telling you," Tia said, "it's not a parlor—"

"Please, Tia," Vickie coaxed. "Maybe you can make it work."

Slowly, Tia sat down and put her fingers on the pointer.

That creepy feeling came over Darcy again. *It's just the shadows in here,* she told herself, *and the eerie, flickering lights. That's what's making me—*

"You're pushing it!" Vickie squealed, interrupting Darcy's thoughts.

"No, I'm not," Tia protested. "It's the table, talking to us."

"Hi," Molly chirped. "I'm a table!"

"Sh-h-h!" Tia hissed, her brow furrowed intently. "This is serious!"

The pointer moved to the letter *D* and stopped. Then it moved to the letter *A* and finally to the letter *R*. Then it stopped moving. Darcy stared at it, her skin prickling.

"Is that all there is?" Vickie asked, sounding disappointed. "Why did it stop?"

"It stopped because that's all there is," Tia replied. "D-A-R, Dar," Molly said. "Hey, Darcy, that's you!"

She lowered her voice and gave it a quaver. "The Great Switchboard in the sky has a message from the beyond—with your name on it."

Tia looked up, her green eyes serious. "Molly's right. The spirits are asking for you, Darcy."

21

Darcy laughed to cover her nervousness. "Anytime I want a message from the beyond, I can turn on cable TV and get something from the satellite."

"Come on, Darcy," Vickie begged, "The spirits are just getting warmed up. There's bound to be more."

Molly giggled. "Yeah, Darcy, how can you resist? Ouija even knows your name."

Darcy looked down at the table. Something inside her warned her to be careful. And yet, at the same time, the table held a fascination she could hardly resist. *It's only a game,* she told herself. *What's there to be worried about?* She reached for the pointer. "Okay, Mol, you win," she said lightly. "I can feel the switchboard cranking up." She placed her fingers opposite Vickie's.

Nothing happened. Nothing except that her fingers felt tingly, as if an electrical current were passing through them from the pointer.

Finally, Vickie sighed. "I guess we might as well—"

The pointer started moving. It circled and then stopped at the letter *R.*

Molly leaned over the board. "You're pushing it, Darcy."

"No," Darcy whispered, "I'm not." The

hair rose on the back of her neck. The pointer was moving again, tentatively at first, then firmly. *E.*

Darcy shook her head. "I'm quitting," she said. But when she started to pull her fingers back from the pointer, it began moving again. *G.*

"You can't quit!" Vickie cried. "We're getting something! E-G . . ."

N was the next letter. There was an odd lightness in Darcy's head, and the tingling in her fingers had reached her elbows.

"I'd better write this down," Tia muttered, and pulled a scrap of paper and a pencil out of her purse. The pointer moved faster, pulling Darcy's hands with it. *A, D.* Then it moved to a blank area and stopped.

"Read it back, Tia," Molly instructed.

"R-E-G-N-A-D," Tia spelled out. "Regnad."

"Regnad?" Vickie asked, puzzled. "What's that?" She squealed. "Wait, there's more! It's moving again!"

T-V, the pointer indicated. Suddenly it slid from Darcy's fingers, and she pulled them away. *The tingling's stopped too,* she thought. *Like somebody turned off the electricity.* She laughed nervously. "Regnad TV? Sounds like a reggae music special on TV. Maybe it's an advertisement."

"Are you okay, Darcy?" Vickie asked. "You look a little white."

"How can you tell, with all that make-up?" Molly asked. She snapped her fingers. "Hey, it could be some sort of message for Tia."

Tia frowned worriedly. "For me?"

"Yeah, sure," Molly said. "You know, T.V.—as in Tia Villette."

"Maybe *regnad* is a Cajun word," Vickie said. "Tia's Cajun, you know," she confided. "Her grandmother came from Louisiana. She's a Cajun witch. Tia says she taught her a lot of spells and things."

"No kidding?" Molly asked.

"What Vickie says is true. I am a white witch," Tia confirmed.

"A white witch?" Darcy asked curiously. She stared at Tia.

"A white witch is somebody who uses her magical powers to help other people," Tia explained. "And it was handed down to me by my grandmother." She paused. Her green eyes were full of—

Of what? Darcy wondered, watching her. *Awe? Fear? But why should Tia be afraid of me? Is it because of what I told her about being psychic?*

"Part of being a white witch is recognizing when others have the power," Tia said

24

quietly. "It isn't something that can be proven, exactly. It can only be felt. I feel it about you, Darcy. I think you have the power—although you may not believe just yet. You may not know how to use it yet, either."

Darcy felt uncomfortable. Tia was right about one thing at least—she didn't know how to use whatever she had. "Sure," she said, gesturing at the Ouija table. "It takes a lot of power to string together some letters that don't make any sense!"

"We don't know that it's nonsense," Tia shrugged. "We just don't know what it means—*yet*. And even if it doesn't mean anything, it could be that the communication just wasn't clear enough and the message got jumbled."

Tia's words hung in the air. The room seemed hot and stuffy, and Darcy pushed herself away from the table.

"I've had enough for one night," she said, standing up. "I'm going to find Freddy Krueger and get him to take me for a romantic walk on the boardwalk."

Molly grinned. "Whistle up The Headless Horseman," she said, "and I'll go along."

The boardwalk was deserted except for the four of them. They moved along slowly, talking. Scott had taken off his mask and razor-fingered gloves, and he held Darcy's hand. Kenny filled Molly in on the latest news of her horse, Ebony, which she boarded at Foxfire Stables, and the two of them made a date to go riding the next week. After a while Scott and Darcy wandered towards the dunes, watching the moonlight spill silver over the quiet ocean. Darcy shivered in her thin black dress. Scott put his brown felt hat on her head and pulled her close.

"Quite a party," he said. "I still don't believe the Masons. It's like they're acting in one of their own movies."

"Yeah," Darcy said. "I keep expecting somebody to roll a camera through the door and yell 'Places, everybody!'"

"Got your Actors Guild dues paid up?" Scott asked with a chuckle. "You could audition for Witch of the Ouija board."

Darcy looked up at him. "How'd you know about that?"

"I came into the room and saw Tia get your name," Scott said. "I was about to ask you if there were any messages for me, but this guy came up and started telling me about his part as a junior vampire in *Son of Dracula Two*."

Scott looked at Darcy, catching her uneasy expression. "Oh, come off it, Darcy. You don't really believe in that stuff, do you?"

Darcy flared. "Yeah, well, I can see that a by-the-book cop might have trouble with something a little out of the ordinary," she said. "Facts, ma'am," she added mockingly. "Just give me the facts."

Scott chuckled. "Yeah, well, facts have an unfortunate habit of biting you when you're not looking."

Darcy had to laugh. "The fact is that my message was a commercial for a reggae special on TV. Don't miss it."

"At least you didn't get something weird like 'Help! Freddy Krueger's got me in his razor-sharp clutches!'" Scott said, putting his arm around Darcy's shoulders.

"Or 'Starving, send sandwiches,'" Darcy laughed, "and no address."

"Speaking of starving, I didn't get any dessert," Scott pointed out.

"Yeah," Darcy said. "Working that Ouija board made me hungry, too." Scott turned Darcy around, and they headed back towards the party. Darcy grinned, feeling a lot more comfortable. *R-E-G-N-A-D T-V. Well, if that's a message from the beyond, I don't have to worry about getting it wrong,*

27

she said to herself. *Wherever it came from, whoever sent it, they royally screwed up.*

But Darcy could never resist an unfinished crossword puzzle or an unanswered question, and she couldn't help trying. *R-E-G-N-A-D T-V,* she spelled out in her mind. *Was it actually possible that the letters had some kind of meaning, as Tia insisted they did? Was it a message for Tia, as Molly suggested?*

If so, what could it possibly mean?

TWO

"How ya doin'?" Darcy asked, setting her tray on the table in the university cafeteria. It was Monday, and she was having lunch with Tia and Vickie after her criminology class, which had been especially interesting that day—Professor Aaron had previously assigned them to read Portland newspapers from the past couple of years and to make a list of the crimes reported in them. Today they had begun discussing their findings: Robbery turned out to be the most prevalent crime, with sexual assault and car theft running close seconds. Many of the crimes hadn't been solved yet.

Tia opened a carton of milk. "Okay, I guess," she said.

"Actually, she's worried," Vickie confided.

"That Ouija board stuff?" Darcy guessed,

with a look at Tia. She pulled out a chair and sat down.

"Hey, you really are psychic," Vickie replied with a laugh. "Since the message had Tia's initials on it, she called her grandmother and asked her what 'regnad' meant in Cajun."

"What did she say?" Darcy asked.

Tia shrugged. "Granny couldn't think of anything, so she told me to make an herb amulet."

"An herb omelet?" Darcy asked, raising her eyebrows skeptically. "What good is that supposed to do?"

Vickie laughed. "Not an omelet," she said. "An amulet. It's magic."

"It's a charm against evil," Tia explained. She pushed back her red-brown hair and fingered a small leather bag around her neck. "Since I don't know what the word means, I used a lot of different herbs, figuring one of them ought to work." She ticked them off. "Feverfew, to protect against sickness. Rosemary, to keep me from having an accident. Rowan, to ward off evil psychic powers. Garlic, against—"

"Vampires?" Vickie asked, wide-eyed. "You're not really worried about vampires, are you?"

"You'd be worried too," Tia said, her

green eyes defiant, "if those were your initials."

Darcy took a bite out of her tuna salad sandwich. Part of her—the skeptical part—wanted to laugh at Tia's amulet, which was probably nothing more than simple folk remedies. But another part of her couldn't help feeling that there was more here than there seemed to be. She could feel how deadly serious Tia was about all this, how deeply she believed. "What else did your grandmother teach you?" she asked.

"How to do spells," Tia said gravely. "How to use herbs and stones, how to make magical incense." She touched Darcy's arm. "She also taught me to recognize psychic power, Darcy. You have a great gift, but you have to learn to respect it— before you can use your power."

Vickie shook her head with a laugh. "You've got to forgive Tia," she told Darcy. "She goes off the deep end with that magic stuff most of the time. If anybody can tell you whether you're really psychic or not, it's Professor Cassidy. He's the psych prof I told you about. He's an expert."

Darcy lowered her sandwich. "An expert on ESP?" *Maybe that's what I need,* she thought. *Somebody who can tell me what all this is about.*

Vickie nodded, her blue eyes shining. "He's even written books about the subject. He detected my ESP right away."

Tia gave a patient sigh. "Vickie, don't you ever get tired of talking about Cassidy?"

"Nah," Vickie said brightly. She smiled at Darcy. "Dr. Cassidy's got a research lab right here on campus. He tests people for ESP. It's really interesting." Her eyes were dreamy. "And *he's* fantastic."

"As in gorgeous," Tia translated, "if you like the slightly older type."

"Oh, yeah?" Darcy asked, interested but wary. She had the feeling that Vickie's enthusiasm might come from a giant crush she had on the guy. "What kind of tests does he do?"

"He had me guess some cards and choose numbers out of a machine," Vickie said. "That kind of stuff. I'm going to the lab this afternoon for another session. Maybe you should stop by there sometime. I know he's always looking for new subjects."

"Maybe," Darcy said slowly, finishing her sandwich. She wasn't sure she liked the idea of someone poking around inside her head, even an expert. It gave her a funny feeling, as if he'd be testing for some fatal disease. *But if I get tested*, she thought, *maybe I'll find out more about this psychic stuff. Maybe I could learn to control it, or at least tune in to it better.*

Tia was frowning at Vickie. "I wish you'd stop hanging around that lab," she said. "I've got a weird feeling about it, like it's bad for you, or dangerous or—"

"Dangerous?" Vickie gave her a scornful look. "What can happen in a university research lab?" She shook her head, narrowing her eyes. "If anything's dangerous, Tia, it's that witchcraft of yours. You know, I really worry about you sometimes. I just read about a bunch of Satanist witches in Pennsylvania who—"

"If they were Satanists, they weren't witches," Tia retorted sharply. "At least, not white witches. We use magic for healing. Satanists are power-hungry. They use magic to push other people around." Tia leaned forward, a concerned look on her face. "All I've got to say, Vickie, is watch yourself. I've got this feeling that there's something wrong about—"

"Then why don't you do a magic spell to fix it?" Vickie asked with a teasing smile. She pushed her tray back. "Hey, how about if we go over to the music store?"

The girls got up from the table and took their trays to the conveyor belt. They were walking out of the cafeteria when Darcy bumped into a custodian bent over a bucket with a mop in his hand.

"I'm sorry," she said automatically.

The man straightened up. "Zaporra" was embroidered on his shirt pocket, and he was probably in his mid-thirties. "Hey," he growled, "didn't you girls see that sign back there? It says 'Wet Floor, Keep Off.'" His voice rose and a red stain crept up his neck and then up his thin face towards his receding hairline. "Just what do you think you're doing, tracking across my wet floor?"

"Hey, I said I'm sorry," Darcy said, feeling the temper rise in her throat. Who did this guy think he was?

Vickie stepped forward. "Well, hi, Chuck," she said in a friendly voice. "Did I ever thank you for giving me a ride the other day? You really saved my life."

Zaporra seemed to calm down a little. "That's okay," he muttered gruffly. "I don't need any thanks." He scowled at Darcy and Tia. "But you better stay off my floors, you hear?"

As the girls walked away, Tia looked at Vickie. "How'd you meet that guy, Vickie? He's a major creep, always looking at girls, like he—" She shrugged. "Well, you know."

Vickie shifted her books. "Chuck's not so bad," she said. "My car died in the ferry lot a couple of weeks back, and he gave me a lift. I kind of feel sorry for him, actually. He lives all alone on the island. I don't think he has any friends."

Darcy looked at her watch. "I guess I don't have time for the music store, guys. I've gotta head for English. Dr. Parnell gets ticked off if anybody comes in after she's started to lecture."

"Speaking of English," Tia said to Vickie, "are we going to work on that Shakespeare project tonight? We only have until Wednesday, you know."

"I haven't forgotten," Vickie said emphatically. "If I had to do that thing by myself, I'd be dead. Why don't I come over after dinner—about seven or so?"

"Sure," Tia said. "You can stay over if you want, and we'll head to school together in the morning."

"Okay," Vickie said. "After all, it could take all night!"

Darcy turned to Tia. "Hey, do you guys mind if I catch a ride with you in the morning? Mrs. Mason's car is in the shop, and she might need the one I'm driving. I'd rather not get stuck driving their hearse!"

"No problem," Tia said. "We'll pick you up about eight. I've got Anthropology at nine."

Darcy started down the hall, then turned around with a grin. "While you're in the music store," she called back, "how about checking the reggae section? Maybe Regnad is the name of a band."

When Darcy grabbed her books and her coat and ran out to Tia's little red Honda the next morning, Tia was alone.

"Where's Vickie?" Darcy asked as she climbed into the car.

Tia was gripping the steering wheel so tightly, her knuckles were white. "I don't know," she said in a steely voice. "She didn't show up last night." She shifted into gear and headed for the ferry. "I'm worried."

Darcy frowned. "Do you think she forgot?"

Tia shook her head. "Not Vickie. She was really worried about that project." Her voice was tense. "We've been working on it for the past couple of weeks, and it's due tomorrow. She was planning to stay all night." Her mouth tightened and she swung the wheel, turning the car onto the beach road. "But she didn't go home either,

36

Darcy. Her parents have been calling since late last night, asking if I've heard from her."

"Didn't go home!" Darcy shook her head. Vickie didn't seem like the kind of person to just disappear. "What do you think, Tia? Does she have a boyfriend she might have stayed with?"

Tia turned the corner. "Not Vickie. She's not that way, Darcy. You know that look she has? Kind of sweet and trusting?"

"Yeah," Darcy said. "Sort of like an innocent little girl."

Tia nodded. "Well, that's the way she is. She told me she went out with this guy named Carl Sanders last year, but he's at Princeton now so they hardly see each other. Guys ask her out all the time, but she's always busy with school and stuff." She gave Darcy a sideways glance. "If you were missing, I wouldn't worry. I mean, I would, but I'd figure that you could take care of yourself." Her voice thickened. "But Vickie isn't like you. She's never been on her own and she's so—you know—*young*."

Darcy sat back against the seat. Tia's concern was contagious, and Darcy began to feel anxious, too. But as they pulled into line for the ferry, she reminded herself that there was nothing they could do.

"My classes are over at noon today," Tia said, taking a ticket from the ferryman. "How about you? Want a ride back?"

"Yeah, sure," Darcy said. "Thanks."

It was nearly twelve-thirty by the time the two girls met again, at Tia's car. Tia looked even more worried than she had that morning. "I called Vickie's dad just before my last class," she said. "Vickie hasn't shown up yet."

Darcy opened the door and climbed into the Honda. "No word, either?"

"Nope," Tia said. She stuck the key in the ignition. "I'm going to her house. Can you come with me? I know you don't know Vickie all that well, but—"

"I'd like to come," Darcy assured.

Back on the island, it took less than ten minutes to drive from the ferry to the Thomases', a tidy gray salt-box house on the bluff above Dune Beach.

Darcy recognized the woman before them as Virginia Thomas, a reporter for KTPM-TV in Portland. *Sure*, she realized, *Vickie must be her daughter. They look alike.* On television, Virginia Thomas was a vivacious blonde. She had the same fragile blond beauty in person, even in jeans and a gray sweatshirt, but she didn't look vivacious just now. Her pale face was drawn and lined with worry. But her eyes held a smile when she saw Tia.

"Tia!" she said hopefully. "I'm glad you've come."

Tia put her hand on Darcy's arm. "This is Darcy Laken. She's a friend of Vickie's, too. We came to see if we could help."

Mrs. Thomas nodded. "Come in, girls won't you?" she asked.

As they followed the woman into the living room, the phone rang. A tall, gray-haired man jumped for it like a drowning man reaching for a lifeline.

"Yeah?" he demanded brusquely. "What've you—" He listened a moment, clutching the receiver. "Yeah, thanks," he said finally. "Officer Phillips, is that the name? Okay, we'll be waiting for him." His voice was dull, as if the life had gone out of him.

Mrs. Thomas took a step forward. "Clark?" she asked frantically, her face a mask of fear. "Clark, what is it? What's happened?"

Clark Thomas turned to his wife. "They've found the car, Ginny," he said. "At Nicky's convenience store at Beach-front and Shore Road. The keys were in the ignition, and Vickie's purse was on the seat. The police are sending a patrolman here to pick up a photo."

Mrs. Thomas stepped forward. "But Vickie?" Her voice was edged with fear. "What's happened to *Vickie?*"

Mr. Thomas shook his head and reached for his wife's hand. "There's no sign of her," he said. "They think she's been kidnapped."

Ten minutes later, Scott was there, crisp and efficient in his blues. If he was surprised to see Darcy, he didn't show it. After hellos and introductions, he took a statement from the Thomases and from Tia. Then the Thomases gave him a photo of Vickie and a description of what she'd been wearing when they last saw her—a short blue plaid skirt, a white turtleneck, and a blue sweater.

"We've put out an APB," Scott told them, "and a search team with dogs is getting ready to fan out from the convenience store."

"A search team?" Mrs. Thomas asked eagerly. She turned to her husband. "I'm going with them, Clark."

Mr. Thomas frowned. "We're both going. But somebody's got to stay here. If Vickie can get to a phone, she'll call here first."

Mrs. Thomas turned to Tia. "Well," she said. "It looks like there's something you can do after all."

"I'll stay," Tia assured her eagerly. She looked at Darcy. "Do you mind walking home?"

"I'll give you a lift," Scott said, pocketing his notebook. "Let's go."

A few minutes later, Darcy and Scott were in Scott's police car, headed for the Mason house. "Pretty hard on the parents," Scott said, cornering the squad car expertly.

"Yeah," Darcy said. She turned in the seat to look at Scott, blond and solid, muscular under his uniform blues—dependable. He was a terrific guy, somebody she could always count on, somebody she could confide in.

"What do *you* think happened to her?" she asked Scott.

Scott shrugged. "Maybe she ran off with a boyfriend," he said. "According to her parents, she isn't dating anybody right now. But parents don't always know."

"Tia doesn't think she'd do that," Darcy said. "She says Vickie wouldn't go anywhere without telling her parents. But there *was* somebody last year. A guy named Carl Sanders. But he's at Princeton."

"Thanks," Scott said, turning the corner at the Masons's road. "I'll check him out."

Darcy could see the house ahead of them at the top of the hill, a spooky old Victorian with crooked shutters. It gave most people the creeps, but Darcy thought it was cool. Besides, she was used to it by now. The Masons had actually "fixed it up" that way. They liked it the way it was—ghost-like. If they changed it, she'd heard Caroline Mason say, the ghosts might go away and not come back. And then where would they get their ideas for horror plots?

"If she didn't go off under her own power," Scott was saying, "there's only one possibility left. She was—"

"She was kidnapped," Darcy said.

"Yeah," Scott said thoughtfully. "And what's really weird is that something like this happened—"

"Just about six months ago, wasn't it?" Darcy asked. "A girl's car was found abandoned at a Portland drug store?"

Scott's blond eyebrows went up quizzically. "Yeah, how'd you know?"

"I had to do a survey of Portland crimes for my crim class," Darcy said. "I remember that one especially, because she was about my age and I thought it was spooky that it was never solved."

Scott gave Darcy a confirming look. "You're right, it wasn't. The girl's name was Marsha Grant. The case is still on the books—open. There was no sign of struggle, no indication of foul play, not a clue to go on." He pulled up in front of the Mason house and switched off the ignition.

Darcy put her hand on the door. "I think I'll change and join the search," she said.

Scott leaned towards her and put his fingers gently on her cheek. "Listen, you be careful. You hear?"

"Right back at cha," Darcy countered blithely.

"What?" Scott asked. "I'm supposed to be careful, too?"

"You got it."

"But I'm a cop!" Scott protested. "Besides, I'm always careful."

"And I'm not, huh?" Darcy asked.

Scott grinned. "Yeah, I know you, Laken. 'Danger' is your middle name." His grin faded. "But whoever's picked up Vickie is a real sicko. He's not somebody you'd like to invite to your house for fun and games. It's that impetuous part of you that I worry about, you know. The part that goes jumping into things without looking at the downside."

"Duly noted," Darcy replied solemnly. "I will be a model citizen." She had her fingers crossed.

THREE

After several hours of searching on foot, the wind picked up and it began to rain. Darcy and Mr. Thomas had brought ponchos, but Mrs. Thomas was unprotected. Soon Mr. Thomas took her home to dry off. He returned without her to the command center the police had set up in the parking lot at Nicky's convenience store. Tia was right behind him. She got out of her car just as Darcy arrived, cold and footsore.

"No word from Vickie?" Darcy asked Tia.

Tia shook her head. "No sign of her out there anywhere?"

Darcy leaned against the hood of Tia's car, pulled off her shoe and shook out a rock. "Nothing," she said wearily. "We've searched the whole area and haven't found a thing." She gave an exasperated sigh. "God, I feel so helpless."

Tia looked at her. "There's something

else we can do, Darcy," she said. "Besides searching, I mean."

"Something else?" Darcy asked.

"Yeah," Tia said, climbing back into her car and leaning over to open the passenger door. "Get in."

When Darcy was buckled in, Tia started the car. "Where are we going?" Darcy asked warily. "And what can we do that the cops and the searchers can't?"

"This isn't a 'we'," Tia said, shifting into gear. "This is a 'you'. And you know what you can do. You don't need me to tell you." She drove off, heading toward the ocean.

Darcy sighed. She knew what Tia was talking about. *Tia wants me to use my psychic ability to look for Vickie*, she thought. *But I've never done anything like that before. Every time I've gotten a flash of some kind, or a dream, I didn't ask for it to happen. I don't even know if I can!*

They drove for a while in silence. Finally, Tia stopped on a bluff overlooking the sea. She switched off the ignition. The sky was leaden, the ocean was a heavy green, and the white surf tumbled noisily onto the rocks below.

Tia reached into the back seat. "Here," she said. She held out a round mirror, six inches or so in diameter. The background was painted black so that the mirror looked deep and shadowy.

"What's this?" Darcy asked, taking it in her hand.

"It's called a scrying mirror." Tia looked hard at Darcy. "It's very old. It belonged to my grandmother. I want you to use it to find Vickie."

Darcy thrust the mirror back at Tia. "Thanks but no thanks," she said. "I know you believe in it, and that's okay for you. But magic isn't my thing."

Tia looked at her. "Are you sure you know what magic is?"

Darcy bit her lip. "Maybe not. I just know—" She looked at the mirror in Tia's hand. "It's not for me, that's all. Whatever this . . . this ability is that I have, I know it's not magic."

Tia's mouth hardened. "I'm not taking no for an answer, Darcy. You have a gift, a powerful gift. Even if you hadn't told me about your dreams and intuition, I could sense it myself, just being with you." She put the mirror back in Darcy's hand. "The searchers didn't find Vickie, and the cops aren't even convinced that she didn't run off. If anyone can find her, you're the one."

The mirror felt warm in Darcy's hand. *It's like it has some internal source of energy,* she thought. Darcy felt her eyes drawn to it, and it took an effort not to look down. "This psychic stuff," she said in a low voice, "I can't trust it. Sometimes I'm right. But sometimes I'm way off the mark." *That's the worst part,* she thought, *never knowing whether I'm right or wrong. Never knowing whether I should trust the way I feel or forget about it.*

"That's because you don't know how to use it," Tia said reasonably. "When I first started doing spells, I couldn't control my power, either. It was a long time before I learned to focus and concentrate my energy. That's the hardest part of the craft, you know. Learning to use your gift. My grandmother says it can take a lifetime."

Darcy shook her head. *All this witchcraft stuff,* she thought, *it sounds so unreal. How can somebody as intelligent as Tia actually believe that she can change anything just by waving her hands and chanting a few words?* But at the same time, Darcy knew that there were many things in the universe that she could never explain—her own psychic ability, for instance. She glanced down at the mirror. There seemed to be a light in its black depths. With an effort, she pulled her eyes away. "If you're so big on this . . .whatever it is, this scrying . . . why don't you do it?"

A giant breaker smashed into the rocks farther up the beach, and the wind whipped sand against the window. Tia looked out of the car window for a moment, then looked back. "I did," she said.

"So?"

"So nothing." Tia's voice was flat. "I can't always trust my power, either. Sometimes it works, sometimes it doesn't. I'm probably letting my feelings about Vickie get in the way of seeing clearly." She bit her lip. "If you're too involved, if you care too much, it doesn't work. And I care a lot about Vickie. She's my friend. I haven't been able to pick up a thing from this mirror."

Darcy sighed. She knew that Tia felt about Vickie the same way she felt about Molly. *And I'd do anything for Molly,* she thought. *Including magic, if I thought it would work.* Against her will, Darcy's eyes were pulled back to the mirror. The light in its depths was definitely brighter now, and there seemed to be an opening deep within it, like the aperture in a camera lens. She looked away.

"How's this thing supposed to work?" she heard herself asking.

Tia gave her a half-smile. "You just look into the mirror and let your mind open. That's all there is to it." She put her hand on Darcy's arm. "Please, Darcy," she said urgently. "I know you think this is so much bull, but I'm not asking you to do it for me. I'm asking you to do it for Vickie."

Darcy let out her breath. *It is probably a total waste of time,* Darcy thought, *but Tia is so intense about it . . . she won't chill out until I've given it a try. Anyway, what can it hurt?*

"Okay," she conceded.

Tia opened the car door and they both got out. The wind swept across the headland, whipping Darcy's long black hair into her face. She stood still as Tia walked around her, drawing a circle in the sand.

"Sit there," Tia told Darcy, pointing to a rock in the middle of the circle. "I've cast a circle. This circle and my chant will create a safe space for you. A space between the worlds, sort of, where alternate realities converge."

Darcy sat down, feeling skeptical. It was one thing to have flashes of knowing, to dream about the future. It was something altogether different to make circles and say chants. *If this isn't mumbo-jumbo,* she thought, *it's something awfully close.*

50

Tia picked up four smaller rocks and turned and walked to the cliff's edge, facing east. "Powers of the world," she called, "we invoke and call your wisdom." She traced a sign in the air—Darcy counted five points—then put down a rock. She walked around the circle and repeated the incantation at three other points—south, west, and north—putting down a rock at each one. Then she raised her hands.

"The circle is cast between the worlds," she called. "The ritual has begun." She stepped outside the circle, leaving Darcy hunched on the cold rock, the wind slapping sand and salt against her.

For a moment, nothing happened. And then it seemed to Darcy that within the circle, the wind died down. She could see Tia's hair whipping into her eyes where she stood beside the car. But where Darcy sat, the wind seemed to have less force.

She looked down at the mirror. The light was there in its black depths. It lured her into the mirror. Time seemed to stop, and she had no idea how long she sat in the still vastness, her eyes on the shimmering light. Then she felt as if she were leaning over the edge of an open well, staring into its black depths with a silvery light dancing on the dark water far below. *The light,* she thought, *it's beautiful. I want to touch it.*

And then suddenly she was falling into the well, into the darkness, toward the silvery light. She was falling, falling, and the light was dying, fading to a shimmery gray and then to nothing—to darkness. Suddenly Darcy felt afraid. She was still falling, into darkness so icy cold and airless that she couldn't breathe. Terror gripped her. Her arms were pinned to her sides by the force of her fall and she couldn't move. But the worst of it was the awful fear, the helplessness, the horror, the overwhelming sense of evil all around her.

She gave a muffled cry. Suddenly she felt the wind pushing hard at her again, and she heard the crashing of waves and the mewing of gulls. Tia rushed up and knelt beside her.

"Are you all right?" Tia asked. "You look—"

"I'm okay." Darcy tried to take a deep breath, but her lungs hurt so much she couldn't breathe. The daylight hurt her eyes, as if they'd been bandaged for a long time and someone had suddenly exposed them.

"Where's Vickie?" Tia asked urgently. "What's happened to her?"

"I don't . . . know," Darcy managed. "I couldn't see . . . couldn't . . ." She shook her head. "It's awful, Tia," she whispered. "I felt so much fear and helplessness! It was all black, and so cold." She shivered.

"What should we do?" Tia asked.

"I don't know," Darcy said hopelessly. "I really don't know." *It's like all the other times,* she thought helplessly. *I get a flash, a feeling, but there's nothing to go on. No information, nothing solid.*

A few minutes later, they were back in Tia's car, driving towards the Masons's house. "At least we know Vickie's alive," Tia said as she pulled up out front.

"How do you figure that?" Darcy asked wearily. Her bones felt achy, as if she had the flu, and she was still cold.

"Because you tuned in to her," Tia replied. "That's the way the mirror works. It was Vickie's feelings you were feeling."

Could that really be true? Darcy thought with a shudder. *It's one thing to feel that horror for a minute, and then turn it off. It would be unspeakably awful to feel it for a long time, for hours and hours, never knowing when it would end. Is that what Vickie's feeling?* She bit her lip. *But maybe the feeling*

I got had nothing to do with Vickie. Maybe it was just— "How do you know it came from Vickie?" Darcy asked.

"I just know," Tia replied. "I feel it. Here." She put her hand over her heart and looked searchingly at Darcy. "Do you believe me?"

"I guess," Darcy said.

Tia nodded. "Before you go, I want you to take this." She picked up the round mirror and held it out.

"No," Darcy said firmly, shaking her head. "I don't want any more of that mirror. Or what's in it."

But Tia's mouth was set. "You have to take it, Darcy. I know it's not the only way to reach Vickie, but it's the best one I know about. We don't know if the cops will find anything. So far they haven't." Darcy's shoulder bag was on the floor at her feet and Tia picked it up and stuck the mirror inside. "I'm putting it in your purse. Okay?"

Darcy managed a small smile. "Do I have any choice?"

Tia grinned. "Not unless you want to deck me."

Darcy had to laugh at that. On her first day of high school, she had punched out Marianne Reed, her longtime nemesis for

54

calling her "white trash." Darcy had never forgotten the terrific sense of satisfaction she'd felt—even if it was only momentary. "It wouldn't be the first time," she said, opening the door to get out.

"Somehow I didn't think so," Tia said.

It was nearly five o'clock when Darcy walked up the stairs. Molly was in her pink and white bedroom at the end of the second-floor hall, finishing a session with Judith, her tutor. Next term, Molly would be back in high school, but she'd missed a lot of work after her accident and Judith was helping her catch up.

"You're doing great, Molly," Judith said, closing the book. She glanced at her watch. "Hey, I've gotta go. I promised some friends I'd go bowling with them tonight."

Molly looked at Darcy, her round eyes worried. "Any news about Vickie?"

Feeling tired and bedraggled and still shivering, Darcy sat down and pulled off her sneakers. "Nope," she said. She closed her eyes wearily. She wanted to talk to Molly about what had happened on the beach, but she couldn't—not while Judith was there. "Not a shred," she said. "No ransom demand, either. It's just like it was with that girl in Portland last year."

"What girl?" Molly and Judith asked in unison.

When Darcy told them, Judith shook her head. "Maybe we'd all better be looking over our shoulders," she said worriedly. "Must be a maniac hanging around out there."

Molly made a face. "I guess that's one advantage to being stuck in this thing." She thumped the arm of her chair, her voice bitter. "Who'd want to kidnap a crip?"

Darcy looked at her. The Molly she'd gotten to know so well faced up to her situation with energy and spirit. But sometimes she needed to let her anger out.

"Kidnap a crip?" Darcy asked, considering the idea. "Yeah, sure, I'd do it. In fact, you'd be my first victim. You couldn't get away, so I wouldn't have to tie you up— just jam your wheels." She tossed her head, grinning. "Anyway, your folks are famous. They'd pay big bucks to get you back."

"Are you kidding?" Molly asked wryly. "They'd pay big bucks to get rid of me. In fact, they'd hire a kidnapper, plot the whole thing, then write it up and sell it to the studios. They'd call it something like *Horror on Wheels*."

"Maybe," Darcy conceded thoughtfully.

"But then you'd be famous too. So what're you bitching about?"

Judith eyed the two of them, shaking her head. "I'm outta here," she said, picking up her books. "Who wants to hang around and listen to you guys crack sick jokes?"

"Who said we were joking?" Molly asked as Judith headed for the door. "If I turn up missing, send the cops after Darcy." She raised her voice as Judith left the room. "And tell my dad that if he doesn't pay the ransom, I'm going to come back and haunt him! On second thought," she added as the door closed, "don't tell him that. There's nothing he likes better than being haunted. He'll never pay. My kidnapper will be stuck with me forever."

Darcy sat on the bed, laughing. *It feels good to laugh,* she thought, *after the horrible day I've had, tramping through the underbrush and peering into mirrors.* Then she sobered. *But what kind of day has Vickie had?*

Molly looked at her. "How's Tia doing? And Vickie's parents?"

"About like you'd expect," Darcy said. She pulled her knees to her chin and wrapped her arms around her legs. "Tia stayed at the Thomases', pacing the floor and waiting for the phone to ring. Vickie's parents helped with the search."

Molly closed her eyes briefly. "God, it's awful to be in this chair," she said. "But it's nothing, compared to what it must be like to be kidnapped. Vickie is such a—" She shook her head. "—such a sweet kid."

"She's a year older than you are."

"In years, maybe," Molly said. "But I got the feeling the other night that she's been sort of protected. Like maybe nothing bad has ever happened in her life. If that's true, then it must be terrible for her to realize that people can do really bad things to other people."

Darcy nodded, thinking. *Maybe, ironically, it was Vickie's innocent trustfulness that had made her attractive to somebody—somebody sick. And Molly's right—that innocence could make it even harder for her to cope with what's happening to her.* Darcy remembered with a sick shudder the terrified helplessness she had felt that afternoon when she'd looked into the mirror. *If you don't know how to roll with the punches, even a tap can be a knock-out.* She hesitated. "Listen, Mol, will you promise not to laugh if I tell you something?"

Molly screwed up her face. "Is it funny?"

"Not that kind of funny," Darcy said, and she told Molly about her freaky experience with Tia's scrying mirror.

"It isn't funny at all," Molly said. "It sounds kind of scary. I don't know if I buy all that magic of Tia's, but it sounds like you could've tuned into Vickie's feelings. The trouble is, it doesn't really get us anywhere."

Darcy nodded, agreeing. "Tia says it means that Vickie's alive, but—"

"But maybe she's already dead, and the feelings you were getting were like . . . delayed."

"Yeah, right." Darcy shivered. *Is that what it feels like to be dead? Dark, cold—*

Molly gave her a quizzical look. "Or maybe you're really getting through to Vickie but she can't tell you where she is because something's blocking the transmission. Or because she doesn't know."

Darcy sat up. "Yeah," she said. "I didn't think of it that way, but it sounds right. Maybe she's just so overwhelmed by what's happening to her that fear and confusion are the only feelings she has. And if she doesn't know where she is—"

"You know what all this means, don't you?" Molly interrupted.

Darcy looked at her. "What?"

"It means," Molly said, "that you'd better

59

take another crack at that mirror. Maybe Vickie will get herself together enough to figure out where she is. Or maybe you'll be able to get through whatever is blocking the transmission."

Darcy sucked in a quick breath. *Experience those feelings of helplessness again?* "God, Molly, I don't—"

"Yeah, I know," Molly said sympathetically. She looked at Darcy. "So when are you going to do it?"

Darcy let out her breath in a long sigh. *I hate to, but I have to. For Vickie.* "Tonight, I guess," she said.

"Can I watch?"

"I'd rather you didn't," Darcy said apologetically. "I mean, I feel kind of weird anyway, sitting there looking into a mirror and waiting for it to talk to me. With you watching, it'd probably never work."

Molly nodded. "Yeah, well, I can understand that. Listen, if you call Vickie and she answers, give her a message from me, huh?"

"What's that?"

She grinned. "Hang in there. The cavalry's coming."

Darcy waited until the Mason house had quieted down for the night—well, until it was relatively quiet, because the old house creaked and groaned all night long. Caroline and Gomez joked that the noises were from the ghost of Gomez's mother chasing his father around the attic. Darcy wasn't sure if they were pretending or whether they thought it was really true. She'd gone up to the attic once. It was full of dusty cobwebs and clumps of hanging bats, and there were several large trunks among the piles of boxes and old newspapers—trunks big enough to conceal Grandma and Grandpa Mason. Darcy hadn't looked inside them.

Tonight, she sat by her bedroom window for a long time, looking out. The trees were a moving lacework of black against a round white moon, and the shadows beneath were pools of darkness. Somewhere, an owl gave an eerie call. Darcy shivered. *Vickie, where are you?* she thought. *What's happened to you?*

Could the answer to her questions really lie in the mirror? Darcy got it out and held it, trying to remember what Tia had said about why the circle was important. *What would happen if I try to use the mirror without casting a circle?* she wondered. *What would happen if I try to cast a circle and get it wrong?* She sighed. Maybe it would be safer to forget about the circle.

She looked down at the mirror in her lap. *Nothing. Just black. See? Nothing there,* she told herself. *All that crazy stuff that happened was just your—*

No, there was something. The light. Darcy pulled in her breath. Just a pinpoint of light. But then it grew into a round, silvery circle. For a moment Darcy looked into it, and then she felt herself stepping into it, stepping through it, almost like Alice through the looking glass. And behind the mirror was a room—the Masons's family room, crowded with people, just as it had been on Saturday night, except that nobody was moving. They were all frozen, like statues. And as Darcy walked among them, suddenly she saw herself, sitting at the Ouija table across from Vickie, both hands frozen to the pointer.

The Ouija table. She leaned over and looked at it. The pointer was moving across the board, tracing the outlines of large red letters, red as blood. But it wasn't R-E-G-N-A-D T-V this time. Now the letters spelled V-T D-A-N-G-E-R. *Why?* she asked herself with a frown.

Of course! she answered her own question. *It's because I'm looking at the scene in the mirror. The letters are in reverse order!*

And then, as Darcy stared at the reversed lettering, she knew the truth.

What the Ouija board had given her that night really had been a message, a warning. But it wasn't for Tia—it was for Vickie. V.T.—Vickie Thomas.

FOUR

When Darcy went to class the next day, everybody was talking about Vickie's disappearance. The Thomases had appeared on KTPM-TV news, asking for help in finding their daughter, and the television station was offering a big reward for any information about Vickie's disappearance. Volunteers were combing both the mainland and the island.

"What gets me," one of the girls in Darcy's criminology class said when Professor Aaron brought up the case, "is that there hasn't been a ransom demand."

Darcy shifted in her seat. "Yes, but there was never a demand in the case of that other missing girl," she pointed out. "—Marsha Grant. Maybe the kidnapper isn't out for money. He could be some kind of weirdo." *A sex weirdo,* she thought. *And if that's true, Vickie really is in danger.*

"I knew Marsha," a boy said from the back row. "She was in my psych class."

Darcy turned around, surprised. "She was a student here?"

"That's right," Professor Aaron said. He paused. "For a detective, this could be a lead—the fact that both girls were students here, that is."

"I didn't know her, but if you ask me," another girl said, "this Vickie person just decided to blow it off. Finals are coming up before too long. I'd be outta here myself, if I wasn't going to graduate at the end of the semester."

A few kids laughed. But before Darcy could tell them what she thought of people who made half-assed jokes about a kidnapping, a red-haired guy spoke up from the front row.

"I think they ought to bring in a psychic," he said. "You know, like they did in that case in Massachusetts."

Darcy forgot about being pissed. "What case in Massachusetts?" she asked.

Professor Aaron leaned on the podium. "A six-year-old boy was abducted from a playground last year," he said. "At the request of the family, a psychic was brought in—a woman who had worked with the police before, incidentally. Within a week, the child was found, unharmed, only a few miles from where the psychic had indicated."

"The way I heard it," the red-haired guy said, "the parents gave the psychic the kid's favorite sweater. She got messages from it or something." He grinned. "Weird, huh?"

Not so weird, Darcy thought. She grinned wryly to herself. *But I'll bet you'd really freak if I told you about getting a message from an Ouija board—backward. And then seeing it straight in a mirror.* "Do the police use psychics very often?" she asked the professor.

Professor Aaron laughed. "It takes an open-minded police officer to accept information that comes through a psychic. The police are more interested in verifiable data. After all, they have to build a case that will hold up in court and convince a judge or jury. Most judges and juries are skeptical about psychics."

The boy next to Darcy spoke up. "My psych professor isn't skeptical—Professor Cassidy. He writes books about psychics and ESP."

Darcy sat up. *Cassidy,* she thought. *That's the professor Vickie was so high on.* She'd forgotten all about him.

Professor Aaron nodded. "I didn't mean to suggest that psychic information couldn't be useful in solving a crime," he said. "I just meant to point out that the police are suspicious of it, and it's very difficult to introduce psychic information as evidence in a court of law." He looked at his watch. "I'm sorry to break up this interesting discussion, and I hope we hear some good news about Vickie Thomas soon, but we're running short of time. If you'll turn to page—"

Darcy opened her textbook. *Cassidy, huh?* she thought. *Well, maybe that lab will be my next stop.*

After class, she turned to the guy beside her. "Do you know where I can find Professor Cassidy?"

"Yeah," the guy said. "Try the basement of Lamont Hall. That's where he's got his lab."

Before heading back to her car, Darcy stopped by the lab and talked to Professor Cassidy's assistant, a graduate student named Frieda. She made an appointment to be tested the very next day.

Later that afternoon, Darcy, Tia, Molly, and Kenny joined the volunteers helping the Sunset Island police force search for

Vickie. The search had expanded to the south end of the island, but without any luck. At about twilight, it began to rain. Kenny took Molly home in his van, Tia went over to the Thomases' house to see if there was anything she could do, and Scott and Darcy headed for the Play Café.

As they walked in, Scott put some coins in the old-fashioned Wurlitzer, and they found a table as an old Elvis Presley song, "Love Me Tender," began. It was a song that had always made Darcy feel sad, and now, wondering where Vickie was and what had happened to her, she felt very depressed.

She and Scott ordered burgers, soft drinks, and fries.

When the waitress left, Scott took Darcy's hand in his. "It's really terrible, isn't it," he said. It wasn't a question.

Darcy looked down at Scott's hands on hers and felt comforted. "Yeah," she said. "I just wish there was more I could *do*."

He squeezed her hand tightly. "Hey, you're doing what you can. You were out there beating the bushes all afternoon."

"Yes, but I'd like to do more." Darcy paused. "Scott, have you ever been on a case where the cops used a psychic to get information?"

Scott released her hands. "Nope," he said. He leaned back. "And if it's up to my sergeant, I never will."

She remembered what Professor Aaron had said that morning. "Look," she said, reading his expression, "I know you're a cop who—"

Scott's face was intent. "I'm a cop who respects your intuitions, Darcy. I've seen you in action, remember? But I have to be honest. I'm still pretty wary of the psychic stuff. And I have to live with Sergeant Murphy—and with the facts. The fact is, solid, systematic police work turns up concrete data. That's what solves crimes and convicts criminals. Psychic information can help, in the right situation. But—"

Darcy leaned forward. "Don't you think this could be the right situation?"

Scott grinned, but Darcy could see the tension in his jaw. "I don't know," he said quietly. He looked at her. "Are you going to tell me that you've got some information about Vickie?"

Darcy bit her lip. "Nothing specific. I mean, I can't tell you where she is. But I have the feeling that she's alive."

Scott's eyes narrowed. "Is it just a feeling or—?"

"It's just a feeling," Darcy said regretfully. "I wish I could tell you something more solid. But maybe I'll be able to before long." She told Scott about Professor Cassidy and his psychic research work. "He's an expert. From what I hear, he's written a lot of articles and books on the subject. I made an appointment at his lab to get tested for psychic ability tomorrow."

And I'm also hoping, she reminded herself, *that this expert can help me use the gift I have. For all I know, Tia could be right—it could be Vickie's only chance!*

"Good," Scott said. "I hope you get what you want from this guy." He propped his chin on his hands and looked at her seriously. "These psychic flashes of yours—it isn't that I don't believe in them, Darcy. It's just that . . . well, in order for me to use that kind of information in police work, there has to be something real, something I can see, hear, smell, taste—"

"Yeah," Darcy said dryly. "Well, I want to know what Vickie is seeing and hearing right now. I want to know where she is. And if there's any way I can get that information, I'm going to do it!"

FIVE

The next morning, Molly drove herself and Darcy in her specially equipped van to the university campus. At the insistence of Dr. Erickson, her neurologist, Molly had signed up for a physical therapy program at the university swim center. But she went begrudgingly, as she was still apprehensive about aligning herself with other physically challenged people.

"Who wants to spend the morning floating around a swimming pool with a bunch of crips?" she asked bitterly.

"I don't know," Darcy said, looking out the window at the chilly gray sky. "It might be pretty nice. Maybe you'll meet some new people. And you've got that terrific new bikini. With your bod, it really looks great."

"You mean, this bod with the legs that don't work?" Molly said acidly.

Darcy decided it was time to shut up. When Molly was in one of her moods, sometimes it was better to let her work it out on her own.

She was right. By lunchtime, when she and Tia met Molly in the cafeteria, Molly's spirits had lifted.

"Hi, Molly," Tia said. "How're you?"

"Water-logged," Molly said, tossing her still damp brown hair. "But this is one therapy I don't mind. You should see the therapist." She rolled her eyes. "Six feet, blond, muscles, and absolutely gorgeous. A real knock-your-eyes-out babeasaurus. I'm thinking of telling Dr. Erickson to double my dosage."

Darcy and Tia laughed. "Sounds like you had a good morning," Tia said. She pulled a chair back and sat down. In a more somber voice she asked, "Hey, are you two going to join the search this afternoon? We finished with the beach area yesterday and now we're working our way into the dunes."

"What are you looking for?" Molly asked.

Tia's face tightened. "Anything," she said. "Clothes, something that might have belonged to Vickie, a body—" She broke off.

Darcy cleared her throat. "I'd like to come," she said, "but I have to talk to

74

Professor Cassidy's research assistant. And after that, I thought I'd drop in and see Mr. and Mrs. Thomas."

"Oh, yeah?" Tia looked at her quizzically.

Darcy nodded. She had a reason for going to the Thomases', but she didn't want to get Tia's hopes up unneccessarily.

"Can I come to the lab, too?" Molly asked. "I'm curious about this guy."

Darcy started on her lasagna. "Sure, if you want. The tests might be pretty interesting."

Tia frowned. "I know you think I'm being silly, but I've got a bad feeling about that lab. Something's going on there that—"

"I wouldn't worry so much, Tia," Darcy said. "Dr. Cassidy's supposed to be one of the best in his field."

"But you can't always trust the experts," Tia objected. She leaned forward, her eyes intense. "Look, you guys, all I have is a feeling, and maybe that's not enough for you. But I really wish there were some way I could talk you out of doing this."

Molly laughed and pushed her tray away. "Don't sweat it, Tia. Even if that lab was full of rattlesnakes, you couldn't keep Darcy away. She's hoping that Cassidy can help her decode some of the messages she's—"

"Messages?" Tia looked at Darcy. "As in more than one? Did you use the mirror again?"

Reluctantly, Darcy nodded. In this brightly lit cafeteria, with kids laughing and trays clattering, her trip through the looking glass seemed like a bizarre dream. She'd told Molly about it, but she wasn't sure she wanted to go into the details with Tia.

But Tia was insistent. "So what happened? Come on, Darcy, this thing with Vickie is making me crazy. It's all I think about, day and night. Tell me what happened when you used the mirror."

Darcy pushed her plate away. "The bottom line is that the Ouija board reversed the message," she said. "Like in a mirror. You were right, Tia. It *was* a message. But instead of being R-E-G-N-A-D T-V, it was supposed to be VT DANGER."

"V.T.! Vickie Thomas!" Tia breathed. "Of course! Darcy, that's terrific! You see? I knew you were the one who could—"

"What's so terrific about it?" Darcy asked with a shrug. "So now we know who the warning was for—kind of late, isn't it? And even if we had known the warning was for Vickie, we wouldn't have had a clue what kind of danger she was in."

"Well, maybe," Tia said. "But the mirror—"

"The mirror didn't bring us any closer to finding Vickie," Darcy said firmly. "It didn't cough up a special delivery letter complete with return address, did it? Hey, if that had happened, I'd be banging on your door, pleading with you to make me an apprentice witch!"

Tia shook her head, her green eyes pleading. "Please, Darcy, don't give up. The cops don't have a clue. And the searchers haven't found anything. Your contact with Vickie may be our only hope of finding her!"

"Who's giving up?" Darcy asked. "Why do you think I'm seeing Professor Cassidy? Having somebody poke around inside my head isn't my idea of a fun way to spend the afternoon, you know." *It's the truth,* she thought with a frown. *There's a part of me that wants to find out about this psychic stuff, from a scientific point of view. And that wants to learn how to use it better. But there's another part that feels—well, weird. Like maybe this is something I shouldn't be fooling with.* The apprehension was nothing that she could put her finger on, and it didn't have anything to do with black magic. But all the same, there was something about being tested that made her feel uncomfortable.

Tia nodded reluctantly. "Well, okay," she said slowly. "But just to be on the safe side, I'm going to make an amulet of magical herbs to protect you. I'll make one for you, too, Molly. Will you wear it?"

Molly looked doubtful. "Will it smell?"

"Like wild flowers," Tia promised with a smile. She turned to Darcy. "And I'm making some of my grandmother's incense for you, to burn when you use the mirror again. It's made of cinquefoil, chicory root, and clove. It'll clear the atmosphere of evil influences and enhance the vibrations."

Darcy shrugged. "I guess it can't hurt," she said. "But I'm not promising to use it—or the mirror."

"That's okay," Tia said, "you don't need to promise. But I want you to have it, just in case."

"Just in case Darcy decides to apply for her apprentice witch papers?" Molly asked. She grinned. "What about it, Tia? Is there a special witch uniform? Will she have to pay dues?"

"Right," Darcy said. "How much does it cost to join the witch union?"

Tia leaned forward and touched Darcy's arm, her face earnest. "I've got big news for you, Darcy Laken. You don't have to be a witch to have the power. You've got it already—like it or not! And all the ESP experts in the universe aren't going to change that. It's something you'll just have to learn to live with."

"Darcy Laken," Darcy told Frieda, the petite, dark-haired girl sitting at the computer terminal in Dr. Cassidy's office.

"Sure," Frieda said. "I remember you." She handed Darcy a clipboard. "Please put your name down on the log, and the date." She looked at Molly. "Are you together?"

"I'm Molly Mason," Molly said. "Would it be okay if I took the test, too? I probably don't have ESP, but I think it's interesting."

Frieda smiled. "Of course," she said. "We have room on the schedule today. In fact Dr. Cassidy likes to have a full range of data represented in his preliminary sample. But the complete testing program and consultation are only available to those with a high score on the preliminary test."

As Darcy handed the clipboard to Molly, she saw with a start that Vickie's name was on it. The date was Monday, the day of her disappearance. *But of course,* Darcy reminded herself, *Vickie said she was coming here after lunch.* She shivered. *What happened after she left? Where is she now? Will we find her in time? Before—* She made herself stop. It was too horrible to think about.

When Molly finished signing in, Frieda took out a sheaf of papers. "Before we begin the preliminary testing," she said, "I need to tell both of you about Dr. Cassidy's research and its importance."

Darcy leaned forward. Frieda said Dr. Cassidy's name with the same reverence that Darcy'd heard in Vickie's voice. *This guy must be pretty impressive,* she thought. *Either that, or Vickie and Frieda both have a crush on him.*

Frieda began to recite information as if she had memorized it. "As you may know, extrasensory perception is the ability to see and understand things without using our ordinary senses—sight, hearing, and so on. Most people have some degree of ESP. That is, they get hunches, have sudden insights, and so on, although they often forget these things almost as soon as they happen. Some people, however, have a much higher level of extrasensory perception. They're the ones Dr. Cassidy wants to identify through the preliminary tests. When he finds these highly psychic people, he gives them more tests to see exactly what kind of extrasensory skills they are using. He also uses several special training techniques—including hypnosis—to enhance and focus their abilities."

Hypnosis? Darcy frowned. Vickie hadn't said anything about being hypnotized. *I'm here to get control over my ability, not lose it. Anyway, I'm pretty stubborn. If he can't hypnotize me, will Cassidy refuse to work with me?*

"With training," Frieda concluded, "people often find that they can summon these skills on command, rather than waiting for extrasensory perceptions to occur randomly."

"Sort of like training a dog," Molly commented flippantly.

Frieda didn't catch Molly's sarcasm. "Sort of," she said, "although of course it's far more complicated than that." Her voice became soft. "Dr. Cassidy is a wonderful, caring person. He makes the experience very pleasant."

"How do you know?" Molly demanded.

"Because I'm one of Dr. Cassidy's research subjects," Frieda said, "as well as his lab assistant. Being in this project is the most exciting part of my life. I love it."

"But does it work?" Darcy asked bluntly. "My reason for coming is to learn to use what I've got, whatever it is. I don't mind being one of his subjects, but if the project doesn't help me, I don't have time for it." She thought of Vickie. *Especially now, I don't have time.*

"Well, a lot depends on your personality," Frieda said. "Some people benefit enormously from the program. Take me, for instance. Before, I kept having intuitive flashes, but they weren't specific. I'd get a kind of hunch about something, but I never knew what it meant."

"Yeah, that's me," Darcy said. "I get messages, but they're all mixed up. And even if my hunch is clear, I don't know whether I can trust it." She thought of Molly's accident. "And there's another thing. Say I see something. Does that mean it's going to happen, regardless? Or can the future be changed?"

"That's one of the questions Dr. Cassidy is trying to answer," Frieda said, her eyes sparkling. "And if he does, the whole scientific community will benefit. His research is very important, probably the most important of its kind in the United States, maybe in the world! He even got a commendation for excellence from the National Research Council." She took out two questionnaires. "If you'll fill these out," she said more levelly, "we'll do the tests."

It took only a few minutes for Darcy to fill in the blanks with the standard information—name, age, social security number, health record, number of brothers and sisters, and so on. There were other questions, too: where she was living now, with whom, the names of her boyfriend, her friends, the names of her pets.

"Why would they want all this personal stuff?" Darcy wondered out loud.

"Who knows?" Molly shrugged. "Maybe they use it later, in the experiments or something."

After a few minutes, Frieda looked up. "All done?"

Darcy nodded and handed her the questionnaire. Frieda stood up. "Okay, Darcy," she said, "you can come with me." She turned to Molly. "This will take about forty minutes," she added. "There's a soda machine down the hall."

"If you're bored," Darcy said, "you could go over to the pool and hang out with your therapist."

"Now there's an idea," Molly said, her eyes brightening.

Darcy followed Frieda through a door, down a dark, narrow hallway, and into a brightly lit room. Darcy saw a computer and printer, something that looked like a bingo cage filled with numbered Ping-Pong balls, and several other strange-looking pieces of equipment.

Frieda sat down at a table and motioned for Darcy to take the chair opposite her. She opened a drawer and pulled out a pack of playing cards and a scoresheet. "I'm going to lay out cards, one at a time," she said, "face down. Look at the card, then guess it. I'll keep track of your guesses on this score sheet." She shuffled the deck several times, put it face down on the table, and placed the first card in front of Darcy.

Darcy looked at it for a moment, trying to imagine what was on the other side. Nothing came to her. Finally she called out a random card—"Ace of hearts."

Her face impassive, Frieda looked at the card, then noted something on her sheet.

"I was wrong, huh?" Darcy asked.

"I'm sorry," Frieda said, "didn't I tell you? I can't reveal your success rate. If Dr. Cassidy wants you to know, he'll tell you himself—if you pass the prelims."

Darcy sighed. *I'll have to do better than*

this if I want to get into the project, she thought. But when the card test was over, the whole thing was a bust as far as she could tell. Sometimes she had a hunch, but never anything very strong.

It was the same thing with the bingo cage.

"There are fifty numbered balls in here," Frieda said. "I'm going to blindfold you. You call out a number between one and fifty and turn the crank on the cage. Then take out a ball and give it to me. I'll write down the number and put it back. You'll have fifty tries. Okay?"

"Okay," Darcy conceded. "I hope I do better this time. Though I was always a bust at bingo. . . ." She tried to at least bring humor to the situation.

But doing it blindfolded wasn't any fun, either. By the time she fished fifty balls out of the cage, Darcy was getting bored with the whole thing, especially because Frieda seemed to be taking it so seriously. She tried making a joke or two, but Frieda only made polite noises and went on with the testing.

Darcy raced through the third test, which involved predicting the colored shapes that appeared on flashcards. The final test was done on the computer. Sets of six randomly generated numbers came up on the screen and Darcy had to guess the three digits that weren't there. By the time the last number set was finished, she was ready to throw in the towel. It was impossible to assess her performance, not having had any feedback, but she surely didn't feel confident. She followed Frieda out of the room feeling dejected.

"If you'll take a seat in my office," Frieda said, "I'll test your friend."

Darcy and Molly traded places. Darcy got a root beer and opened her English book. *While I'm waiting,* she thought, *I might as well finish my assignment.* She had just started to read a short story called, "The Yellow Wallpaper" when the door opened and Chuck Zaporra—the maintenance guy they'd run into earlier that week—came in with a fluorescent bulb in one hand and a ladder over his shoulder.

"This where I'm supposed to change the light bulb?" he asked, in the same surly tone Darcy had heard before.

"I don't know," she said. "Frieda's the one you need to talk to. She's giving a test right now. I don't think you'd better go back there."

Zaporra leaned his ladder against the wall and examined the lights in the ceiling.

"Well, it sure as the dickens isn't in this office," he said disgustedly. "Must be in the back somewhere. And this is the second time this week I chased over here to replace it." He scowled. "Tell Frieda if she wants that bulb changed, she's going to have to write up a work order."

Darcy frowned. *The second time this week?* "You weren't here on Monday afternoon, were you?"

Zaporra gave her a dark look. "What if I was?"

"I just wondered," Darcy said, tossing her hair carelessly. "If you were, maybe you happened to see this friend of mine. Come to think of it," she added, "she's a friend of yours, too. Vickie Thomas. You know, the one you gave a ride to?"

Zaporra's face shut down. "I don't give rides," he said, hunching his shoulders. His face had a strained, wary look, as if he were afraid of something—and afraid of showing his fear.

"But you did," Darcy insisted. "Don't you remember? You and Vickie talked about it. She said that her car died in the ferry lot and you—"

He picked up his ladder. "Ain't got time to stand around," he muttered. "You tell Frieda to write up a work order. Tell her

I'm not coming back without it." He slammed the door behind him on his way out.

Darcy's eyes lingered on the closed door. *That look on Zaporra's face—what did it mean? And why did he deny giving Vickie a ride?* It was a question that nagged at her as she went back over her English assignment, writing out the answers to Dr. Parnell's questions.

Darcy had just finished the last question when Molly wheeled herself through the door. Darcy looked up. "How'd you do?" she asked.

Molly shrugged. "How am I supposed to know? Poker-Face wouldn't tell me a crummy thing. How'd you do?"

"Same deal," Darcy said. She sighed. "But I know I screwed up. I had a few hunches, but nothing spectacular."

Five minutes later, Frieda was back. She turned to Molly. "I'm sorry to tell you, Molly, that your preliminary score on the screening was just about as high as we would expect from random guessing. You did better when you picked the balls out of the hopper, which suggests that your psychic abilities are stronger when you're in physical contact with an object. But overall, I have to say that your ESP is in the normal range, which isn't high enough to qualify you for the program. I hope you're not too disappointed about not getting to work with Dr. Cassidy." The tone of her voice implied that Molly ought to be disappointed.

Molly shrugged. "How'd Darcy do?"

Darcy shook her head. "I flunked," she said. "I bombed every test."

Frieda smiled. "No, Darcy, in fact, your scores were very high. I can't tell you the actual results, of course. You'll have to ask Dr. Cassidy. I know he'll want to interview you himself just as soon as possible." She went to the desk and opened an appointment book.

Darcy blinked, surprised. *If my ESP is all that good,* she thought, *why didn't I know I was getting the answers? But maybe it doesn't work that way. Maybe, as Tia said, feelings sometimes get in the way.*

"How about tomorrow at eleven?" Frieda asked, running her finger down the column of appointments.

"Sure," Darcy said. "I could stop in after my criminology class."

Frieda wrote Darcy's name down. "I'll see you tomorrow, Darcy. And when Dr. Cassidy reviews these results, I'm sure he'll be very anxious to meet you."

When they had left the lab, Molly laughed. "Woo-woo," she said, mimicking Frieda's tone. "Aren't you just dying to meet the famous, fabulous Dr. Cassidy?" She shook her head disgustedly. "What exactly is the deal with Frieda? All she could do was make goo-goo eyes over him. But if he's such a world-famous researcher, how come his office is in the basement?"

"Who knows?" Darcy asked. She helped Molly negotiate the basement door. "But maybe you're just pissed off because you don't get to meet this guy."

"Forget it," Molly said. "I don't want anybody hypnotizing me." She looked at Darcy. "Are you actually going to let him put you under?"

Darcy shrugged. "If it'll help me get a handle on this ESP thing, I'll play along. But I've got to get something out of it, too—like learning to control this psychic stuff better, and learning how to use it when I want to, rather than just sitting around waiting to get flashes. If I'm lucky, I'll be able to help Vickie before it's too late."

"Yeah, sure," Molly said. She looked at her watch as they came to the corner. "Hey, do you suppose we've got time for a chocolate shake before we head for the ferry?"

"There's always time for a shake," Darcy said. "But then I'd better head back for the island. I want to stop at Vickie's house this afternoon." She eased Molly's chair over the steep curb. This was one of those crossings where there was no ramp for the disabled. *Funny how I notice things like this, now that I know Molly,* she thought. *Before, mobility-impaired people were sort of invisible to me. They made me uncomfortable, so I never looked at them, or their problems.* Darcy made a mental note to call the university about getting the curb ramped.

"How come you're going to the Thomases'?" Molly asked. She looked up at Darcy. "You think you'll find out anything?"

Darcy nodded. "Maybe if I look in Vickie's room, I'll get a clue about where she is." She shivered as the wind bit through her coat, and she thought about Vickie. *Wherever she is,* she thought, *I hope she's warm.* Darcy looked down at Molly. "Hey, Mol, want to come?"

"Yeah, sure," Molly said. "Why? Do you have something you want me to do?"

"Yeah," Darcy said. "Let's talk about it over a milk shake. I've got a plan, and I need you to help."

SIX

Mrs. Thomas answered the door on the second ring.

"How are you, Mrs. Thomas?" Darcy said, looking at Vickie's mother's tired face. "Remember me? I was here on Monday with Tia. I'm Darcy Laken."

Mrs. Thomas was breathless, as if she'd run the length of the house to answer the door.

If only I had some good news to tell her, Darcy wished. "This is my friend Molly Mason," she continued. "Vickie was at a party at Molly's house on Saturday night."

Virginia Thomas's eyes were red-rimmed and puffy, but she gave the girls a weak smile. "Come in," she said, leading them into the living room. "I'm glad you caught me. I have to leave for work in an hour." She turned to Molly. "So you're Molly Mason. Vickie told me she really enjoyed meeting you. I've always been curious about the people who lived at that—"

"That unbelievably creepy old house on the hill?" Molly asked with a laugh. "Everybody's always asking what kind of weird people live there."

Mrs. Thomas's eyebrows arched. "I was about to say that it was a very interesting old Victorian," she replied. "A marvelous example of the kind of house they don't build any longer. I did a television feature on Victorians last year. There aren't many good ones left." Her smile faded and her face grew tight, as if she were trying to keep from showing emotion. "Vickie helps me with some of my features. We're planning to do one on adopted children sometime soon."

She's using the present tense, Darcy thought, *as if she doesn't want to believe that Vickie might be dead.* Darcy sat down on the edge of the sofa. "Molly and I were wondering if you'd heard anything more," she said. "Have the police come up with any clues?"

Mrs. Thomas sighed and shook her head. "Nothing new, I'm afraid. They didn't find any strange fingerprints on the car—and there was no sign of a struggle. They're saying that whoever took Vickie didn't touch her car."

Darcy narrowed her eyes. "That suggests that she was already outside when she was taken," she said. "I mean, it doesn't look like somebody jerked the door open and yanked her out."

"Unless they were wearing gloves," Molly put in.

"But Vickie always keeps the car doors locked," Mrs. Thomas said. She leaned back against the sofa cushions. "A family friend in New Jersey lost his automobile in a carjacking. Ever since then, Vickie's been really careful about locking the doors." She smiled. "In fact, she seemed so worried that her father tried to get her to lighten up. That's when she told us she had a—"

Darcy had a sudden flash of understanding. "She had a premonition about being kidnapped from a car?"

Mrs. Thomas looked at her. "She told you about it too?"

"Not exactly," Darcy admitted. "I'm guessing." *But I'm not surprised,* she thought. *Vickie must have ESP, or Dr. Cassidy wouldn't have included her in his project. Maybe she did have some kind of flash about getting kidnapped.*

Mrs. Thomas nodded. "Vickie's involved

in some kind of ESP research at the university. Her father encourages her." She smiled a little. "They've both always loved to read about UFOs and that sort of thing."

"If she's careful about her car doors," Molly postulated, "then the kidnapper must have been somebody she knew."

Darcy nodded, frowning. "Maybe she got out to talk. That's when they grabbed her and pulled her into another car."

"But Nicky's is a busy place," Molly objected. "People are going in and out all the time, day and night. If somebody grabbed her, she would have struggled, and then someone would've seen it. I mean, it's all over the news—I can't believe no one would come forward."

"Which means she didn't struggle," Darcy said quietly.

Mrs. Thomas passed her hand over her eyes. "The police are saying that she might have gone willingly. But if she did, I'm *sure* she never intended to stay away. She knows how much we love her. She wouldn't put her father and me through this." She swallowed painfully, her eyes misty with tears.

Darcy stood up and gave Molly their prearranged signal. "May I use the bathroom?" she asked.

"Of course," Mrs. Thomas said. She pointed. "It's down the hall, just past Vickie's room."

Molly smiled. "And could I bother you for a glass of water, please?"

Mrs. Thomas got up quickly, as if she was glad to have something to do with her hands. "I'm sorry," she said. "I should have offered you something." She started for the kitchen. "But wouldn't you rather have some hot chocolate? It's a chilly day. And I baked some of Vickie's favorite chocolate chip cookies—in case she comes home."

"Thanks," Molly said. "I'll help." She wheeled herself after Mrs. Thomas.

Left alone, Darcy headed down the hall. But she didn't go as far as the bathroom. Instead, she stopped at the door of what had to be Vickie's bedroom. The walls and carpet were blue. The blue and white bedspread and curtains had dainty lace ruffles, and the small lamp on the bedside table had a blue and white ruffled shade. A bulletin board hung on one wall, plastered with pictures of Vickie and her friends, high school pennants, a prom announcement, even a few faded flowers. On another wall were posters of rock stars and movie stars, hung over a shelf that held Vickie's CD player, discs, and books. Darcy smiled in spite of herself to see Luke Perry's face looking at her. The bed stood against the third wall, and the fourth had two closed doors—a closet, probably, and a private bathroom.

Darcy closed her eyes and stood quietly, hopefully. *Come on, Vickie,* she thought, trying to send out her thought waves like a radio signal. *Can you hear me? Where are you?*

Nothing. Darcy opened her eyes. Not a damned thing. And she didn't have much time. Even with Molly doing her best to distract Mrs. Thomas, it would only take five minutes to put a few cookies on a plate and microwave some hot chocolate. And either way, Darcy's prolonged absence would be noticed soon.

Darcy walked around the room, running her fingers lightly over various objects—Vickie's bulletin board, her pictures, the mementoes of her high school years. Nothing. She continued with Vickie's posters, her CD's, her books. Zip. Darcy opened the door to Vickie's bathroom and went in. Everything was neat and clean—nothing caught her attention.

Back in the bedroom, she opened the closet. *The psychic in the Massachusetts kidnapping had used a sweater to locate the little boy,* she remembered. *Clothes must have a special connection with a person.* Darcy ran her hands over the clothing in the closet—blouses, skirts, pants, dresses, jackets, sweaters. Nothing. About to give up, Darcy buried her face in a jacket and smelled a faint perfume—lily-of-the-valley. It evoked a clear picture of Vickie's china blue eyes and delicate, almost child-like face, but nothing else.

Darcy heard voices in the living room. Mrs. Thomas and Molly were back. She felt she'd better get going before she was caught, or she'd have some embarrassing explaining to do. She stepped swiftly into the bathroom and flushed the toilet for effect. But as she turned to leave the bedroom, she saw something else—stuffed animals and dolls, lovingly arranged on Vickie's bed.

Stepping to the bed, Darcy picked up the animals, holding each one briefly. The first was a striped tiger, its tail frayed, one eye missing. She felt warmed by a feeling of tender playfulness. Suddenly she knew that the tiger had been Vickie's favorite animal—but when she was much younger. *A child, a little girl,* she thought, *dragging her best friend around by the tail.* She put down the tiger and picked up an elegantly dressed doll. *Nothing special here. Maybe it was a gift from somebody she didn't care about.* Darcy touched a tattered Snoopy pillow—again, warm, cozy feelings. She picked it up and held it against her. *Vickie loved this, too.*

As Darcy put the pillow down, she saw that there was something under it. A bear. A saucy brown plush bear with glittering black eyes and a red velvet ribbon—almost new. Darcy picked it up—and gasped.

The feeling that came from the bear was not of warmth or tenderness or love. It was black, cold, and evil. An overwhelming evil that seemed to rush at her in waves, pulling her under, like a heavy surf—

Chilled and frightened, Darcy closed her eyes and took a deep breath. Still holding onto the bear, she forced herself to think logically. *I have to contact Vickie somehow. That's why I'm here.* "Vickie," she whispered out loud, "where are you?"

No answer. Nothing but dark, cold waves of—

Darcy dropped the bear on the pillow; a feeling of hopelessness swept over her. *It's no use,* she thought. Her ESP was working, but what she was getting was too vague to do her any good. *To do Vickie any good,* she amended silently.

Darcy turned to leave Vickie's room. *I have to get some help!* she thought. *I can't deal with this situation alone any longer. Thank God I'm seeing Dr. Cassidy tomorrow. He's supposed to be the expert. He might be able to help. And he knows Vickie, too.*

And if he can't help? another, more skeptical voice asked inside her. *What'll you do then?*

Darcy had to admit that she didn't know.

"So, Darcy Laken," Dr. Cassidy said, from the other side of the desk, "you've done it again." He looked up from the score sheets from tests that he had just given her. "You've blown the top out of our scoring system, not just yesterday, but today as well."

"And is that good?" Darcy asked, studying Dr. Cassidy covertly. She could see why his students would develop crushes on him. His curly brown hair, light blue eyes, white teeth, and a dimple in his right cheek combined to make him one of the sexiest, most drop-dead gorgeous guys she had ever seen. *Probably in his early thirties,* Darcy speculated. And he had such an open, smiling face that any misgivings she might have had were easy to put aside.

Dr. Cassidy threw back his head and laughed, good-naturedly. "Is that good? I don't have extraordinary ESP myself, Darcy, so I have to rely on a scientific evaluation of your skills. What would you say if I told you that you are among the top one percent of the extraordinary people I've tested—during my entire career? And that's raw ability I'm talking about. Why, with a little bit of enhancement—" He shook his head, sobering. "You have an enviable talent, young lady. My task is to see exactly how remarkable it is by measuring it with certain research methods, and to help you develop it properly."

Darcy leaned forward. "How long will that take, Dr. Cassidy? To develop it properly, I mean."

His grin was easy and friendly. "Why? Are you on a tight schedule?"

"Well, yes," Darcy said. "To tell the truth, I'm in the middle of something right now that—" She hesitated. *How much can I tell him?* she wondered.

He cocked his head, his blue eyes intent on hers. "If you're wondering whether you can trust me, Darcy," he said soberly, "the answer is yes." His voice was deep and warm, with an authoritative ring. "I've worked with a great many people, most of whom wanted to keep their abilities confidential. People with your innate abilities don't want to be treated like sideshow freaks. If I include you as a case study in any book I write—and I suspect that I will—I can promise you total anonymity. Unless you tell them, no one, not your relatives or your friends, will know that you've been here." Dr. Cassidy looked down at the information sheet she had filled out. "Not even your boyfriend," he added. "I see that he's a police officer."

"Anonymity isn't what I'm worried about," Darcy said. "It's—"

He leaned forward and gave her an encouraging smile. "You have to be totally honest with me," he said. "If you're not, I won't be able to help you."

She nodded. *He's right,* she thought. *I can't expect him to do much for me if I don't level with him about this.* "All my life I've gotten, well, feelings," she said. "I pick up on people. I know things, intuitively. When this guy I know—Kurt Ackerman—was accused of robbing a house on Sunset Island last summer, I knew he didn't do it. And my friend Molly—I dreamed that she would be hurt in a terrible accident, before it happened." Darcy looked at him. "Do you need more examples?"

"They can come later," he said. "I'll want to get your personal history from you in detail. But for the moment, just give me the overall picture, so I can get a fix on what's bothering you now."

Darcy looked down at her hands, feeling a sudden surge of relief. It felt so good to talk to somebody who understood the whole thing from a scientific point of view. "The trouble is that sometimes my psychic sense doesn't work," she said. "I thought a girl in my high school class had a brain tumor, and she didn't." She swallowed. "I didn't know that Vickie Thomas was going to be kidnapped—and I should have known. I got the message totally screwed up. Backwards, in fact."

"Vickie Thomas?" Dr. Cassidy asked sharply. "You got a message about her?"

Darcy nodded. "On Saturday night we were at a party, and we started playing with this Ouija board. I got a bunch of letters, but it looked to me like nonsense. I got the message straightened out later, when I used a mirror, and found that it was a warning to Vickie. And when I went to Vickie's yesterday I—" She closed her eyes against the memory of the horrible black evil that had engulfed her when she picked up the bear.

Dr. Cassidy reached out and touched her hand. "Whoa, there, Darcy," he said gently. His eyes were comforting. "Obviously, you're very upset." He shook his head sadly. "We're all upset about Vickie. I knew her too, you know. She's a student in my intro class and one of my research subjects. A very bright, capable young woman. I hope she'll be found."

"I think maybe I can find her," Darcy said simply. "But every time I try, all I get are these vague feelings. Nothing specific. Nothing that could really help the police."

"Would you like to try again, using hypnosis?" Dr. Cassidy asked.

Darcy looked at him uncertainly. "How would that help?"

"I'm not sure that it would," Dr. Cassidy admitted. "To be honest with you, hypnosis works best when the subject's personality is—" He grinned crookedly. "Well, a little less assertive than yours. Somewhat less take-charge."

Darcy couldn't help smiling. *He's got me pegged—already!* "In other words, you need a subject who's willing to take orders."

Dr. Cassidy chuckled from deep in his throat. "I don't think I'd quite put it in those terms. Cooperative is the word I'd choose. Hypnosis works best when the subject is willing to cooperate with the hypnotist." The corners of his attractive mouth quirked. "Ordinarily, your strong will might not make you the best subject for a research approach based on hypnotism, Darcy. But you seem to want very badly to use your psychic ability to find Vickie."

"I do," Darcy said urgently. "I want it more than anything!"

"Then it's entirely possible that your wish to help your friend may make you more cooperative than you might be otherwise."

Darcy frowned. *I'm still not crazy about this,* she thought.

The corners of Dr. Cassidy's blue eyes crinkled, and he smiled. "Look, Darcy. The truth is that you won't do or say anything under hypnosis that you believe to be wrong. So if that's what you're worried about, you can forget it."

"If I were hypnotized," Darcy asked slowly, "would it make it easier for me to tune into Vickie?"

"I think it would," Dr. Cassidy said. "You've heard about the two halves of the brain?"

Darcy nodded. "Right and left brain, right? I read about it last year in psychology. The left brain is logic, the right brain is intuition?"

"Exactly. Under hypnosis, the logical left

106

brain relaxes its control and permits the right brain to work without interference. If you allow me to hypnotize you, I'll give you a series of suggestions for relaxing conscious control and for tuning in to your intuition. These will be very simple suggestions, nothing frightening, nothing that will make you anxious. Then we'll see what happens."

Darcy still felt edgy. "What do you think will happen if you hypnotize me?" she asked. "Will I say something?"

"You might. When I sense that we've gone as far as we should for one session, I'll wake you. You'll feel relaxed and comfortable, and you won't remember a thing. That's a precaution," he added, "just in case we should uncover some troubling material that your conscious mind isn't prepared to cope with just yet."

Darcy sighed. *I don't really like the idea of this, but nothing else has worked in finding Vickie. And this guy obviously wants to help.* Dr. Cassidy seemed like the kind of person Darcy could trust. "Okay," she said, making up her mind. "Let's get the show on the road."

"That's what I like," Dr. Cassidy said warmly. "A woman who knows what she wants to do." He pointed to an upholstered sofa. "Just lie down and relax."

Uneasily, Darcy lay down, while Dr. Cassidy dimmed the lights and pulled up a chair beside her. He leaned forward, tucking his tie between two buttons of his faded Oxford and he pushed up the sleeves of his lab coat. The last thing Darcy saw before closing her eyes were the knees of his faded jeans. Then she eased her eyelids shut and rested her head flat on the couch.

Dr. Cassidy began to speak in a low voice. His words were slow and soothing. "Close your eyes, Darcy," he instructed. "Relax and breathe deeply. You'll notice your arms and hands feeling heavy. Your breathing will slow. You will feel very drowsy, very . . ."

Darcy felt her eyes grow heavy. But instinctively, she fought against the odd sensation of letting go of her consciousness. *What would happen if I went into a trance and never woke up?* she thought dimly. *Would I just sort of drift around forever, like a boat without any rudder?* She felt her stomach muscles tighten and she clutched at consciousness.

Dr. Cassidy leaned closer. "You're safe here," he said, reassuringly. "I'm here to help you. There's no need to struggle, no need to resist." His voice became more insistent. "You feel drowsy. Your breathing is slowing."

Darcy could feel her eyelids flicker as her eyes struggled to open. Dr. Cassidy gently touched each of her eyelids, and continued: "Your eyelids are heavy. Your arms and hands feel so heavy you can't move them."

And suddenly, in spite of her resistance, they were heavy. Darcy's arms and hands were leaden, without feeling. She felt a flash of fear, but Dr. Cassidy's voice was so soothing, so reassuring, that it began to melt away, along with her resistance.

"As you listen to my voice, you're no longer afraid, Darcy. You're beginning to trust, you're letting go, you're letting yourself slip into a trance. . . ."

It might have been ten minutes later when Darcy woke up, or three hours. She had absolutely no sense of how much time had elapsed. But as Dr. Cassidy had said, she did feel terrifically relaxed, as if she'd had a wonderful sleep. She wasn't even the slightest bit groggy.

Dr. Cassidy turned up the lights, beaming. "Hey," he said, "you are one fantastic girl!"

"Fantastic?" Darcy asked, pushing herself up on one elbow. "What do you mean?"

"Of course you won't remember any of this," he said excitedly, "but under hypnosis, you were able to give Vickie's kidnapper's name and a partial description!"

"No kidding," Darcy breathed, elated. "Are you sure? I can't remember anything."

"No kidding is right," Dr. Cassidy said. "Obviously, your left brain is working as a blocking mechanism, scrambling some of the perceptual abilities of your right brain. When you're hypnotized, the blocks are removed, and your right brain is able to function to its fullest capacity. And what a capacity!" he was obviously very excited.

"His name," Darcy said urgently. "What did I say his name was?"

Dr. Cassidy looked down at a small notepad. "You weren't speaking very clearly," he said, "so it was a little difficult to decipher. But as nearly as I could make out, it was Keister or Keiver. Something like that." He looked at her. "Are those names you recognize?"

Darcy shook her head, puzzled. *Keister? Keiver? Who can that be?* "I'm drawing a blank. What did I say he looked like?"

He looked at his notes again. "Mid-thirties, thinning hair, narrow face."

She frowned. *There must be thousands of guys who look like that.* "Did I say anything else?" she demanded. "Like, where he's keeping Vickie? Did I say that?"

Dr. Cassidy gave her a smile. "You're a very impatient person, aren't you? Unfortunately, this kind of work is often slow. It takes a while for the subject to relax deeply enough to relinquish control, and there's a danger of overtaxing the system. I'm sure you know more—psychically, that is,—about Vickie's situation than you can tell me during a single session. I'd suggest that you come back again, and we'll repeat the process. Are you willing to do that?"

"Of course I am," Darcy said without hesitation. *At last we're getting somewhere!* she thought jubilantly. *How could I have distrusted him? He holds the key to finding Vickie, I know it!* "How soon can I make an appointment?" Darcy asked.

Dr. Cassidy went to his desk to check his calendar. "How about Monday at one? I know you'd like to get on with this quickly, but we can't do it over the weekend. I've got something else scheduled, and anyway, the lab's closed."

"I'll be here," Darcy promised. She thought about Vickie. It had already been four days! "I can't wait to find out more."

He nodded, his blue eyes warm and sincere. "To tell the truth, Darcy, I am very concerned about Vickie as well. And I am just as eager as you are to find out what you know."

SEVEN

The Sunset Island Police Department was a busy place. A woman with teased blue hair was paying a traffic fine, an overweight man was complaining about a dog, and a patrolman was questioning a couple of punks caught shoplifting in a convenience store. When the woman had paid her fine and the man sat down on a bench to fill out his complaint form, Darcy stepped up to the desk.

"I'd like to see Scott Phillips," she said to the officer behind the desk, a tall, broad-shouldered woman with a brunette page boy. Darcy had seen her before, when she stopped in to talk to Scott.

"Friend of his, aren't you?" the officer asked brusquely. "Is this business or pleasure?"

"This is business," Darcy said firmly. "It's urgent."

The woman raised a dark-brown eyebrow. "Yeah, well, he's off-duty right now. But you might try the break room." The phone rang and the officer gestured with her head as she reached for it. "That door. End of the hall on your left."

The break room was long and narrow, painted institutional green, with a green tile floor. Vending machines lined one wall, sofas and chairs another. A dart board hung on another wall, with what looked like a scoring sheet posted beside it. Over one sofa was a bulletin board filled with notices from various organizations. Scott was sitting on that sofa with his feet on a messy coffee table. He wore street clothes and had a soda can in one hand and a clipboard with papers on it propped against his knee. Two uniformed policemen were sprawled on chairs, talking and drinking coffee out of paper cups.

Scott grinned when he saw Darcy.

"Hi, Darcy." He tossed his soft drink can in a nearby recycling box. "How're you doing?"

"Hi," she said. She looked uncomfortably at the other officers. "Got a minute?"

"Yeah," Scott replied. He gestured towards the sofa. "Sit down, I'm just finishing this paperwork."

One of the other cops looked at his

watch. "Speaking of paperwork, guess I'd better get back to the desk and see if Jake's got that report typed up yet."

The other cop laughed and drained his coffee cup. "Anytime you're ready to turn Jake loose, let me know. My partner doesn't type. I have to do it all myself." The two of them got up, nodded to Darcy, and left.

Darcy took off her coat, sat down on the sofa, and pulled both feet up under her. "Actually," she said, "I'm doing great. I just had this terrific session with Dr. Cassidy."

Scott made a note on his clipboard and put it down. "Dr. Cassidy—that ESP expert at the university?"

Darcy nodded. "He says I'm in the top one percent of all the people he's ever tested."

"Oh, yeah?" Scott asked. He leaned back on the sofa and grinned lazily, his eyes warm and appreciative. "I could have told him that, Darcy."

Darcy smiled back. "But there's more, Scott. When he hypnotized me—"

Scott's lazy grin disappeared. "When he what?"

"When he hypnotized me," Darcy repeated.

Scott looked at her intently. "He hypnotized you?"

Darcy nodded. "You see, Dr. Cassidy's got this really interesting theory. His idea is that the left brain, which is where we do all the logical thinking, interferes with the right brain, which is where the psychic stuff—"

"I get the general picture." Scott leaned forward, frowning. "But hypnotism isn't a game, Darcy. I know it's used a lot. But used in the wrong situation, people can really get freaked out. It freaks *me* out to think of you under some strange man's spell."

"He's not a 'strange man,' and we weren't playing a game," Darcy countered. "Look, Cassidy's a doctor—he's an expert on psychic research. His work has been recognized by—"

Scott put his hand on hers. "I wouldn't care if the guy was knighted by the Queen of England, Darcy," he said, very quietly. "I just don't like the idea of him screwing around with your—"

"He wasn't screwing around with anything!" Darcy insisted, feeling angry that Scott didn't share her enthusiasm. *He's just too protective of me,* she lamented. "Dr.

116

Cassidy was helping me get in touch with the kidnapper, Scott. And I *did*!"

Scott stared at her. "What do you mean, get in touch with the kidnapper?"

"Vickie Thomas's kidnapper," Darcy said.

"Darcy," Scott said sounding worried, "if you've been out there on your own, talking to—"

"I didn't say I actually *talked* to him." Darcy frowned at Scott. "Look. You said you needed something concrete, something factual. And, I've got two facts for you—the guy's name and what he looks like. I'm sorry I didn't get his address, but I guess that'll have to wait until next time."

Scott's voice was calm but his expression vacillated between anger and concern. "Are you trying to tell me that this Dr. Cassidy hypnotized you and you came up with the kidnapper's name and a description?"

"I'm not 'trying' to tell you anything," Darcy said, fighting to be patient. "That's what I *am* telling you. Under hypnosis, one side of my brain relaxed the control it usually has over the other and—"

Scott picked up his clipboard, turned over a sheet of paper, and took a pencil out of his pocket. "Okay, Darcy. So what's the kidnapper's name?"

Darcy squirmed. *I wish I could remember exactly what went on during our session,* she thought. *Next time, I'll ask Dr. Cassidy to use a tape recorder, so I can listen to it later.*

"Well, actually I'm not sure about the name," she said in a lower voice. "It could have been Keister. Or maybe Keiver. Something like that. But I do know that he's in his mid-thirties, with a narrow face and thinning hair."

Scott's pencil was poised. "Well, which do you think? Is it Keister or Keiver?" he asked.

"I don't know," Darcy said. "I don't remember. Dr. Cassidy said my voice wasn't very clear when I—"

"You don't remember? You mean you *forgot?*"

"Scott, I was hypnotized," Darcy explained. "That's part of it. You say things, but when you wake up, you don't remember them."

Scott sighed. "Look, Darcy, I'm not trying to give you a hard time about this. But if you don't remember what happened while you were hypnotized, how do you know what you said?"

"Dr. Cassidy read me his notes from the session," she replied. "It was all right there. Scott, come on, I know the police are doing their best to find Vickie, but what if you find her too late—or not at all—like what happened with Marsha Grant? Don't you understand? If I can do something to help I have to do it!"

Scott jammed his pencil back in his pocket. "Okay, at this point, I'm willing to go with whatever we can get. I'll run a computer check on Keiver and Keister, and any other variations I can think of. And I'll talk to Cassidy and get his statement." Scott leaned forward, his eyes intent. "But I have to tell you, Darcy, I'm going out on a limb with this stuff. Sergeant Murphy doesn't trust psychics. Your word won't be good enough for him unless you score on the name—and even then, it'll be iffy—so don't be disappointed. And the sergeant won't be any too keen on this Dr. Cassidy, either. If any of this is going to fly, we'll have to come up with something concrete that'll convince—"

"The computer search will turn up something convincing," Darcy said. "I'm sure of it." She looked at her watch. "Since you're off-duty, why don't we go get something to eat?"

Scott gave her a regretful smile. "I wish I could," he said, pushing himself up from the sofa, "but I'm taking Jacob's shift to-night. I won't be off until midnight. I'm sorry."

"It's okay," Darcy said, getting up. "Let me know when something about this guy turns up on the computer."

Scott helped her on with her jacket. "You sound pretty confident."

Darcy turned around and met his eyes. "I'm not," she confessed honestly. "I've been wrong too often to be sure about anything. I guess I'm just hoping." *Hoping I'm right so that Scott won't look like a fool for believing me and so I won't look like a fool for believing in myself! And most of all, so we have a chance of finding Vickie!*

Scott leaned over and kissed the tip of Darcy's nose. "Yeah, I'm hoping too," he said.

The wind had turned much colder, and thick white flakes of snow were beginning to fall out of a twilit sky when Darcy drove up to the Mason house. Tia Villette's car was parked in the drive. Simon came out of the dining room as Darcy entered the house.

"Ah, Darcy," he said, rubbing his hands. "It is a lovely night, is it not?"

"If you like wind and snow," Darcy said, stamping her feet.

"Oh, I do," Simon said with morbid delight. "I *do*. Did I ever tell you about the winter I spent in Scotland, filming *The Loch Ness Vampire*? It was the depths of the season, and we stayed in this splendidly drafty old castle which had a resident ghost named Sir—"

"Tell me later, Simon," Darcy said, shivering. "Just the sound of it is making me cold. Where's Molly?"

Simon pulled himself up to his full height, his head grazing the chandelier. "Molly and her guest are in the family room," he said dejectedly, "where I have laid the fire. Do you care to join them?"

Oh, Lord, Darcy thought, *now I've hurt his feelings*. "Thanks, Lurch," she said, and saw his stern, craggy face soften slightly. "A nice warm fire is exactly what I need."

She found Molly and Tia sitting in front of the fireplace, sharing a bowl of popcorn. Tia jumped up when Darcy came in. "I was so worried about you!" she exclaimed.

"Worried?" Darcy asked, bending over the fire to warm her hands.

"Yeah," Molly said, reaching for the popcorn. "She's got the idea that this Cassidy

121

dude is a vampire in disguise, and that he spirited you off to join him in his coffin."

Tia gave Darcy a concerned look. "Did your session with him go okay?"

"Piece of cake," Darcy said. She turned around to warm her back. "Really, Tia, there's nothing to be worried about."

"At least not any more, there isn't," Molly said. She held a closed hand out to Darcy. "Here you are, Darcy. One hundred percent protection, compliments of your local Witchs' Safeguard Society. Tia made one for me, too," she added.

Darcy took it. It was a soft leather pouch on a rawhide thong. It had a faint herbal odor.

"It's the amulet I was telling you about," Tia said. "It's full of good things. I used mullein for courage, snapdragon to keep others from deceiving you, thistle for energy, and sandalwood for protection. I put in a piece of hematite—that's a mineral—to give you strength. And I chanted a special spell at midnight to enhance the effectiveness."

Molly fingered her pouch. "Hematite? Is that anything like kryptonite? Will it make me able to leap over tall buildings in a single bound?"

Darcy grinned. "How about short build-

122

ings?" she asked, hanging the amulet around her neck.

"Actually, I'd settle for curbs," Molly said wryly.

Darcy turned to Tia. "Have you met Professor Cassidy?"

Tia shook her head. "No, but Vickie talked a lot about him. She said he's cute."

"That," Darcy said emphatically, "is the understatement of the century. And the session was terrific." She leaned forward. "When he hypnotized me, I—"

"He actually *hypnotized* you?" Tia put in worriedly. "Really, Darcy, I don't think—"

Darcy ignored her. "I came up with the name of Vickie's kidnapper. It's either Keister or Keiver. I even picked up on a description—thinning hair, narrow face, mid-thirties."

Tia gasped.

Molly's round eyes grew big. "You're kidding," she marveled.

Darcy shook her head. "I stopped by the police station and told Scott. He's going to check the computer and see what he can turn up."

"That's great!" Molly said excitedly. "But where does this guy live? And where is he keeping Vickie?"

Darcy shook her head regretfully. "I

don't know, but I'm going back on Monday afternoon. Maybe we'll find out then."

Tia's face was taut. "Darcy, I wish you'd use the scrying mirror instead. I found a recipe in one of my grandmother's books for a clairvoyance brew. All you have to do is boil some mugwort and bay leaves and cinquefoil in pure spring water, add a little anise oil, and—"

"Bubble, bubble, toil and trouble," Molly intoned in a quavery voice, passing her hands slowly over the popcorn bowl. "Fire burn and cauldron bubble. Make Darcy clairvoyant, on the double."

"Molly, this isn't a joke, you know!" Tia exclaimed. "It's a life and death matter! Vickie needs our help!"

Molly broke off her chant. "Okay, you're right. But I think clairvoyance tea is pushing it. What's she going to do, put it in a thermos and carry it around with her so she can take a sip any time she wants to—"

"She's not supposed to drink it," Tia said, making a face. "She's supposed to *smell* it. It's the steam that does the work. If you inhale it, it helps you enter a clairvoyant state."

"That's what happened under hypnosis," Darcy said. "I didn't need witch's brew for that." She fingered her amulet. "Anyway, I've got this to help me, right?"

"Right," Tia echoed tightly. "Just don't take it off, okay?"

"I won't," Darcy promised, fingering the pouch. "Let's see—you said this is mullein, snapdragon, thistle, sandalwood, and hematite, right?" She frowned. "Haven't you left something out?"

"What?" Tia asked, sounding puzzled.

"Garlic," Darcy said with a laugh. "What if Dr. Cassidy really is a vampire?"

By ten the next morning, the snow had stopped, the sky was clear, and the temperature was rising. Kenny and Molly had gone over to Foxfire to give Ebony a morning workout, and Darcy was about to run some errands, when Scott's squad car pulled up to where Darcy was standing on the driveway. Scott got out and for a minute he just stood looking at Darcy, not saying anything.

"I ran the computer check," he finally said.

Darcy leaned against the car, trying to read his expression. "Well, what did it turn up?" she asked, almost reluctant to hear the answer. Scott's hazel eyes were intent on hers, but she couldn't read what was in them.

"A man named Charles Kleister was arrested in Santa Barbara ten years ago," Scott said. "Attempted kidnapping."

Darcy pulled in her breath. *I was right!* she thought jubilantly. A quick rush of excitement flared through her.

"The victim was a sixteen-year-old girl," Scott went on, his voice tense. "He grabbed her as she was coming out of a drugstore and forced her into his car at gunpoint. They got as far as Ventura before she managed to jump out of the car at a stoplight and flag down a passing motorist."

"A drugstore!" Darcy exclaimed excitedly. "God, Scott, Marsha Grant disappeared from a convenience store!"

"Yeah," Scott said. "It's the same MO, all right. Kleister dumped the car in San Diego, but they got him as he was trying to make it over the border into Mexico."

"This Kleister," Darcy said breathlessly. "What does he look like?"

Scott jammed his hands in his jacket pockets. "Tall, thin. Ten years ago, at the time of the attempted kidnapping, he was twenty-three and already beginning to go a little bald."

"So he'd be thirty-three now," Darcy

said. *Mid-thirties, thinning hair, narrow face.* She felt goosebumps breaking out on her arms. *Aside from the l in his name, I was totally on target, right down to the guy's appearance!* "Where is he now?"

Scott shook his head. "That's the big question. He did five years in San Quentin before they let him out on parole. His parole officer signed him off two years later. According to her, Kleister had relatives somewhere in the Northeast."

"Then he could be *here*," Darcy said quietly. "He could have taken Marsha and Vickie."

"Yeah," Scott said. "He sure could have." His eyes brightened and his mouth quirked in a sudden smile. "I've got to hand it to you, Darcy. You were right this time." He reached out and touched her arm, and his voice softened. "Thanks. I'm sorry if I gave you a hard time. You know how it is. . . ."

"Don't mention it," she said. "You were just doing your job." She glanced at him. "So what's next?"

Scott looked grim. "Next," he said, "we send out the bloodhounds."

EIGHT

Frieda looked up from some papers she was filling out. "Hi, Darcy." She pushed her dark hair out of her eyes. "Dr. Cassidy's in his office waiting for you. He said you had a great session on Friday."

Darcy nodded. "I learned a lot about ESP," she said. "And we got some really important information." She leaned forward. "Do you remember a girl named Vickie Thomas?"

"Vickie? Of course." Frieda's brown eyes saddened. "She was one of the research subjects. I was just devastated when I heard what happened to her. But the worst part is that I had this feeling. . . ." She bit her lip, unable to finish her sentence.

"You had a premonition about Vickie?" Darcy asked. *Sure that made sense. Frieda had said she was psychic, too.*

Frieda fiddled with her pencil. "Just once," she said. "It was when she was signing in, the last time she was here. I had this sudden flash of—" She covered her face with her hands.

"It was awful," she said, her voice muffled. "There was so much darkness, hanging over her in a terrible cloud. I knew I ought to say something to her, warn her. But Dr. Cassidy was standing right beside me, and I was afraid to . . ." She dropped her hands and smiled weakly. "Well, you know. Just in case I was wrong. I'm getting more confident all the time, but still—"

"Yes, I know," Darcy said softly. "The same thing happens to me all the time. I hope Dr. Cassidy's going to be able to help me."

"Oh, I'm sure he will," Frieda said. "He's such a wonderful—"

"Hello, Darcy," Dr. Cassidy said with a smile, opening the door to the hallway. His curly brown hair was slightly disheveled and his sleeves were pushed up as if he'd been working intensely. "Are you ready for another session?"

"Yeah." Darcy nodded. Then she grinned—in spite of her concerns. "But first I have some really exciting news for you. The police checked the computer and found a record of somebody named Kleister. Charles Kleister. It turns out he was arrested for kidnapping a sixteen-year-old girl back in California."

"I know," Dr. Cassidy said. "An officer was here this morning—your friend, I believe," he added archly, "Scott Phillips."

Darcy nodded, surprised by his brief display of emotion. But she discounted her assessment of it when he continued with full composure.

"I was glad to confirm your report," Dr. Cassidy assured her, "and I told him we were having another session today. He suggested that I tape record this one, just in case you're able to bring up any more pertinent information." He smiled at Frieda. "Hold all my calls for the next hour, please, Frieda. I don't want any interruptions. Darcy, why don't we get started?"

"Sure," Darcy said. She turned to wave at Frieda. She was startled to see the research assistant looking at her with wide, frightened eyes. *What's the matter with Frieda?* she wondered.

But the question left Darcy's mind as she followed Dr. Cassidy down the hall into his office. A lot was riding on this session. Scott had called the night before to say that so far the police had turned up a blank on Kleister. No social security information, no driver's license, no nothing.

I have to come up with some new information, Darcy thought as Dr. Cassidy closed the door behind them. *Some way to find Kleister or trace Vickie's whereabouts.* She clenched her hands tightly, until she felt the sting from her nails. *God, I just have to!*

This session began much like the previous one. Dr. Cassidy locked the door to insure that they wouldn't be disturbed, and then he dimmed the lights. This time, he turned on soft music. "It might help you relax," he said, adjusting the volume, as Darcy lay down on the upholstered sofa and made herself comfortable.

Dr. Cassidy sat on the chair beside her and placed a small tape recorder on the end table. "Did you have any more psychic flashes this weekend, Darcy?" he asked. "About anything? About Vickie?"

Darcy shook her head. "I hoped Friday's session might trigger something," she said, "but nothing happened."

"I see," Dr. Cassidy said. His dimple flashed in a smile. "Well, suppose we get started." He bent over and pushed a button on the tape recorder. "Close your eyes, Darcy," he said softly. "Just lie back and let all the tension go. Your eyes are growing heavy. Your breathing . . ."

Darcy relaxed and let Dr. Cassidy's

soothing voice flow through her like a warm wave, gently easing the tension, smoothing the rough edges, softening her, calming her. It seemed easier this time, though at the last moment, she still resisted briefly before letting go. But the dark was velvety-soft and warm, and she felt herself melting into it, Dr. Cassidy's voice was only a low murmur now at the edges of her consciousness.

". . . letting go, relaxing into the dark, getting heavier . . ."

Darcy felt herself sinking into the cushions of the sofa as if there was a weight on her, pressing her shoulders down.

". . . relaxing, releasing . . ."

The warm inviting dark rose up to meet her.

The next thing Darcy heard—how long after she couldn't be sure—was Dr. Cassidy's voice, cheerful and brisk. "Wake up, Darcy," he was saying. "It's time to wake up now."

She opened her eyes, feeling no grogginess, no sleepiness, just instant awareness and a feeling of expectation. "Did I say anything?" she asked quickly, sitting up and running her hands through her hair. "About Vickie, I mean?"

Dr. Cassidy shook his head.

"Nothing?" Darcy asked, feeling frustrated. "You mean, I didn't say anything?" She felt a terrible disappointment, as if she'd somehow let Vickie down—and let Scott and herself down, too. Darcy realized how much she'd been counting on this session.

"You murmured a few words," Dr. Cassidy said, "but there was nothing distinguishable. Here, let me play the tape for you, so you can hear for yourself."

But when Dr. Cassidy pushed the play button on the tape recorder, the tape was blank. "I don't know how that happened," he muttered, sounding perplexed. "I'm sure I turned it on."

"It must have malfunctioned," Darcy said with a sigh. "Like me, sort of."

Dr. Cassidy held out his hand to help her off the sofa. "Well, then, maybe it's a good thing you didn't say anything important," he said lightly.

Darcy straightened her twisted skirt. "I guess that's one way to look at it. But I'd rather have said something about Vickie or Kleister—anything, even if it wasn't recorded."

Dr. Cassidy went back to his desk. "I know how disappointed you are." He leafed through his appointment book. "But psychic work takes time. And even though we didn't learn anything about Vickie, I learned several things that will further my own research—your responses to hypnotic suggestion, for instance."

"My responses?"

Dr. Cassidy sat down in his swivel chair and leaned back, lacing his fingers behind his head. Darcy couldn't help noticing once again how good-looking he was, what a lean, muscular build he had. "May I be frank with you?" he asked.

Darcy sat down across from him. "Please," she said. "Tell me anything you know that will help me understand what's going on with me." *Like, why I connect sometimes, and other times I totally bomb out.*

"You're a remarkable subject, Darcy," he said, "not at all like my other research subjects." He sat up straight and picked up a pencil. "To tell the truth, you present quite an interesting challenge to me—as a scientist, I mean. On the one hand, your strong will certainly makes you more difficult to work with. Even though you're strongly motivated to cooperate, it's just not in your nature to yield control of a situation to anybody else. You don't remember this, of course, but at the last session, it took quite a long time to get you into the trance state. At this session, it was much easier. You were much more cooperative, more willing. But you're still resistant."

"You mean, my left brain won't give up control?"

Dr. Cassidy nodded, turning the pencil in his hands. "I suspect that's why we didn't have the results you were looking for today—although, as I say, I'm quite satisfied with our progress. As a matter of fact, I'm delighted. To a great extent, the success of this kind of work depends on the rapport between the investigator and the subject. I have the feeling we're establishing that rapport, don't you?"

"I guess," Darcy said, "but I still wish—"

"Rapport and trust—those are the two essentials here." He smiled, his blue eyes glinting. "And every scientist knows that although the easy subjects can result in a great deal of data, it's the challenges that lead to exciting breakthroughs. That's what makes scientific history. That's where I feel we're headed, Darcy. This is groundbreaking work we're doing."

Darcy couldn't help feeling a little impatient. Science was fine, but it was knowledge she was after. "I understand that you have your work to do," she said. "But the most important thing for me right now is finding out what's happened to Vickie. That's the only kind of breakthrough I'm looking for—that, and understanding myself. Why I get these flashes, I mean. And why they're right sometimes and other times they're not."

"I know," he said sympathetically. "That's why I'd like to see you again, just as soon as possible." He looked down at his book. "How about Wednesday?"

Darcy leaned forward. "Can't we do it tomorrow?" She clenched her hands, feeling helpless. *Every day's delay makes it seem that much less likely that we'll find Vickie. Time could be running out.*

"I'm sorry." Dr. Cassidy's voice was regretful. "I've got to go out of town tomorrow." His blue eyes were warm and compelling. "Believe me, Darcy, I'd see you if I could. I want this just as much as you do."

Darcy stood up. If he said they shouldn't work too quickly, she would go by that. "Then I'll see you on Wednesday," she said. "Thanks, Dr. Cassidy." She held out her hand.

He took it, holding it briefly. "Thank *you*," he said, and walked with her to the reception room where Frieda was talking to Chuck Zaporra.

It was a tense conversation, to judge

from the look on Frieda's face. "I'm sorry you had to come back, Chuck," she was saying, "but the dean's office didn't have any work-order forms. That's why I didn't fill one out."

"Then tell the dean's office to get them," Chuck growled.

Dr. Cassidy stepped forward. "I'll speak to the dean's secretary myself, Mr. Zaporra," he said. He smiled. "Sorry you had to make an extra trip."

Chuck looked mollified. He hoisted his ladder and headed for the door. "Yeah, well, I was just doing my job," he said. "My boss doesn't like it if I don't do it by the rules."

"We understand," Dr. Cassidy said, as Zaporra closed the door behind him.

"What a jerk," Frieda said angrily. "Next time I'll change the darn bulb myself."

Dr. Cassidy smiled. "He really is a bit of a pain," he said. "But he's just doing his job." He went back to his office.

When he was gone, Frieda gave Darcy a troubled look. "Darcy, I don't know whether I ought to say this, but—"

Darcy frowned, remembering the expression on Frieda's face before her session with Dr. Cassidy. "You flashed on something, didn't you?" she asked uneasily. "Was it about me?"

Frieda nodded. "It was the same feeling I had about Vickie," she said, her voice low and worried. "A terrible, black evil. I wish I could tell you more, but that's all I know. Darcy, you've got to be careful!"

Darcy stared at her. *What had Frieda seen? Was the same dark fate in store for her as the one that had swallowed up Vickie?*

After she left the lab, Darcy headed for her parents' house in Portland. It was beginning to snow when she pulled up. She looked around automatically, checking to see who was hanging out on the nearby corner in front of Santos's Deli. It could be risky to leave a car in the street in this neighborhood, even in broad daylight. When you came back, you could be minus a radio or a tape deck—even minus a car. But she didn't intend to stay very long. And her parents didn't have a driveway to park in—or a garage. There was just the run-down house that Darcy's uncle allowed them to live in, rent-free. The house that Darcy had been glad to leave.

But this afternoon, Darcy's main concern wasn't the sad, shabby house and the crime-plagued neighborhood. As she ran up the familiar ramshackle front steps, she was thinking of seeing her little sister Lilly and her father, Connor. She'd also see Patsi and Patrick when they came home from school, and her mother, Shanna, when she got home from work at five. Darcy had brought a special treat for Lilly from Simon—a giant chocolate cupcake with a cherry on top. Simon was a great baker.

But Lilly wasn't there. "She's gone with Mrs. Collins next door to the clinic," Conner told Darcy in his faint Irish brogue as they went into the kitchen. A big pot of beans was simmering on the stove, filling the gloomy kitchen with its warm fragrance.

"There's nothing wrong with her, is there?" Darcy asked anxiously, shedding her coat.

Darcy's father shook his head. "The clinic was giving free physical examinations," he said, sitting down heavily at the painted wood table that was covered with a too-small oilcloth. "I was going to take her myself, but my arthritis has been acting up again."

Darcy sat down across from him and took Simon's wrapped cupcake out of her purse. "This is for Lilly," she said, putting it in the center of the table. "Have you been taking your pills, Dad?"

Conner Laken nodded. "Sure I have, but

I guess I need another prescription," he said. He was a tired-looking man, his face drawn and gray. But a smile lit up his eyes when he looked at Darcy, and the lines on his face relaxed. "It's good to see you, daughter. How's my college girl?"

Darcy heard the pride in his voice. Her older brothers, Sean and Dean hadn't been able to go to college, and Darcy knew her father took great pleasure in hearing about the university.

"It's great," she responded. "I like all my classes, even Dr. Parnell's English. She gave me an A on my last paper. And I've just been chosen as a research subject in the psychology lab."

Conner got up to stir the beans. "Psychology lab? What happens there?"

Darcy smiled. Her father was a man who believed in things that people couldn't always see. His daughter's psychic abilities had always seemed natural to him. They were simply an extraordinary extension of her ordinary abilities to see and hear. So it was easy to tell him about Tia and the scrying mirror, and about Dr. Cassidy and his research work on ESP. It was more painful to tell him why she had consulted the mirror and had gone to the lab in the first place—about Vickie, and Charles Kleister, and her disappointment at not being able to come up with any new information about the kidnapping during today's session.

Conner frowned when she finished the story. "Aren't you taking an awful burden on your shoulders, child?" He opened the refrigerator and took out a carton of milk.

"What do you mean?" Darcy asked.

He poured milk into her Mickey Mouse mug, the one she'd had since she was a child. "Maybe your psychology professor has a different idea about this, but I think it's asking too much to expect you to be able to come up with such specific information. It isn't something you can just whistle up, you know, like a dog."

"You're saying you think I just ought to sit around and wait until it happens?" she asked.

"You're saying you think you can turn it on whenever you want?" her father countered, sitting down again. There was a slight smile on his face.

Darcy turned her mug in her fingers. "I don't know," she said quietly. "I don't know whether Tia's witchcraft is the right way to turn on my psychic ability, or if Dr. Cassidy's hypnosis is. I only know that we have to find Vickie, and that I'm the only one who's been able to come up with any clues at all."

Her father smiled at her. "You always were too hard on yourself," he said, "and impatient. Even when you were a little girl. You wanted to be the best, to know the most, to be the bravest. And you never wanted to just sit around and let things happen." He shook his head. "I know how you're feeling about your friend, Darcy. But don't let any expert fool you into believing that your gift is something you can pick up and use the way you'd use a computer or a telephone, just because you *want* to—*or* just because *he* wants you to."

Darcy wrung her hands, feeling desperate. He was taking away the only hope she had! "But how can I find Vickie? Tell me how, Dad!"

Conner Laken sighed. "I guess you just wait," he said. "When the time's right, it will happen." There was a smile in his eyes. "I know that's not what you want to hear, daughter. But it's important."

Wait? Darcy couldn't help shaking her head. Waiting wasn't her strong point. *Doing* something was. But she was doing all she could—letting herself be hypnotized, seeking more information—and it wasn't working. What else could she do?

A few minutes later, three-year-old Lilly came in from her trip to the clinic, and climbed happily onto her sister's lap. "A cupcake!" she cried, grabbing it off the table. "It's all for you, sweetheart," Darcy said.

"Can I share it with Daddy?" Lilly asked solemnly.

"Of course you can." Darcy smiled to herself. Lilly had been born after her father's stroke and she instinctively looked after him whenever she could. She never failed to bring joy and amusement to the family.

Lilly looked at Darcy, her head tilted. "Did you lose your button Darcy?" she asked. She chanted one of the nursery rhymes Darcy used to read to her. "Button, button, who's got the button?"

Darcy looked down at her blouse. "Great," she said dryly, "just terrific. Looks like I've been walking around with my shirt half open!"

Her father opened a drawer. "Your mother keeps safety pins here," he said, finding one. He passed it to Darcy. "This is kind of big, but it's all I can find." It was large, with a blue plastic head.

"Thanks, Dad," Darcy said, and pinned the gap in her blouse. "I'll bet that gave the guys a treat," she laughed.

144

"A treat?" Lilly asked, bouncing happily. "Why didn't you just give them a cupcake?"

When Darcy got home that evening it was after eight. The Masons had finished dinner and Molly was watching TV in the family room.

"How'd it go with the great Cassidy today?" Molly asked, reaching for the remote to mute the sound. "Did you come up with anything new?"

"No, nothing," Darcy said, flopping on the sofa. She felt discouraged. "Any developments here? Has Scott called with anything?"

"Not that I know of," Molly said, shaking her head. "Too bad about your session today," she added sympathetically. "I know you were counting on learning something. I'm so worried about Vickie!"

"I know," Darcy said. "Me too. But my father gave me a different slant on it. He says maybe this gift I have can't be programmed. Maybe I shouldn't be trying to learn to control it, to turn it off and on when I need it."

"He could have a point," Molly allowed. She looked at Darcy. "Hey, that's a terrific brooch you're wearing. Tres chic."

"What?" Darcy asked. "What is?"

"That diaper pin on your blouse." Molly pointed. "Are you starting a new fad?"

Darcy laughed. "I lost my button somewhere," she said. She looked at her watch. "I hate to break this up, Mol, but I've got homework."

"Well, I don't," Molly said, reaching for the remote. "Judith decided to relent for a day." She flicked on the sound again. "Talk to you later Darcy."

As Darcy went up the stairs to her bedroom she frowned. *I hate to admit it, but maybe Dad's right,* she thought. *Maybe I shouldn't be trying to turn my psychic abilities off and on like a faucet. And maybe that's why I don't really trust Tia's witchcraft—or, deep down, Dr. Cassidy's hypnosis.* All that sounded like very good advice. But was waiting the best thing to do when somebody's life was at stake?

What would happen if the information came too late?

Or if it never came at all?

NINE

It was nearly eleven that evening. Darcy was finishing her criminology assignment and thinking about climbing into a hot bubble bath when the phone rang. She went out into the hallway to answer it.

"Oh hi, Scott," she said, leaning against the wall. "I tried to call you a while ago, but I didn't get any answer. I wanted to ask what you've found out about—"

Scott didn't let her finish. "I just got off the computer," he said. Darcy could hear the excitement in his voice and could picture his flushed face. "I turned up another piece of information about Charles Kleister. After he was released from parole, he went to Vermont to visit his sister. Just for the hell of it, I ran her married name, on the off chance that he might have used it as an alias. And that's how I found him! Our boy Kleister is alive and kicking.

And what's more, he's living right here, on Sunset Island!"

"No kidding!" Darcy breathed. She sagged against the wall, limp with relief. *I was on the right track! And the computer finished the job.* "What's his name, Scott?"

"Zaporra," Scott said tautly. "Charles Zaporra. And get this, Darcy. He's employed by—"

Darcy felt the breath catch in her throat. She gripped the telephone receiver tightly. "The university!" she said. "He's a custodian there!"

There was a moment of stunned silence on the other end of the line. "Is this another one of your psychic flashes, Darcy?" Scott asked finally.

"No," Darcy said slowly. "I've met him. He's in his mid-thirties, he's got a thin, narrow face, and he's starting to lose his hair. He fits the description exactly! And he's a total creep too, always hanging around, watching people. The women complain he makes them jumpy."

"What about Vickie?" Scott asked. "Did she—"

"You bet she knew him," Darcy said emphatically. "In fact, she told Tia and me that he gave her a ride home a little while back, when her car quit in the ferry parking lot." Darcy bit her lip. *Was Zaporra planning Vickie's abduction when they ran into him outside the cafeteria that day? Did he look at her and think, Yeah, that's the girl I want? Or was kidnapping her something that he did on the spur of the moment?*

Scott let out a long breath. "That's it, Darcy," he said jubilantly. She could imagine the smile on his face. "This is our connection! You've given us the break we've been waiting for!"

Darcy straightened up. "Have you picked him up yet?"

"Not yet, but we're working on it. He lives on the ocean side of the island, about six blocks from Nicky's convenience store. I'm headed over there right now."

"I'm going with you," Darcy said.

"No way," Scott said firmly. She could almost see his lips tightening up, the quick, hard shake of his head. "This could be dangerous. He's bound to be armed. And Sergeant Murphy wouldn't—"

"Screw the danger," Darcy said. "And screw Sergeant Murphy. Don't forget that Zaporra knows me. I might be able to get him to talk. And if he's got Vickie locked up in his house, she's going to need a friend to be there for her." Darcy pulled out her ace: "Anyway, you just said that I was the one who gave you this break. If it weren't for me, you wouldn't even have a suspect, much less know his name and address. I want to be there when you guys show up with the thumbscrews."

Scott was silent for a minute, and Darcy could almost see him rubbing his hand wearily across his jaw. She waited tensely until he finally relented. "Okay, you win." His voice became crisp. "I'll be right over."

The night air was frosty and cold, and the moon was bright silver against a velvet-black sky. Darcy shivered as she went out to the curb to wait. Four minutes later, Scott's car pulled up, tires skidding on the gravel, and Darcy climbed in.

Scott gave Darcy an approving look and a quick grin. "Well, I gotta say that you're a hell of a lot prettier than the guys I usually ride with."

"Thanks," Darcy said. She looked at him, his square shoulders, his well-defined shape. "And thanks for taking me."

Scott cleared his throat. "Yeah, well, I guess you earned it," he said, and pushed the car into gear.

Zaporra's house was near the salt marshes. In contrast to the more affluent part of the island, where many rich and famous people had palatial summer homes, the houses near the marsh were small and ill-tended, and most were in need of painting and repair. A few were nothing but shacks and hovels, and here and there people lived in the rotting hulks of old fishing boats. There were no street lights and no curbs along the oyster-shell roads. Except for a few porch lights, the houses were dark.

Zaporra's small wood-framed house was on a corner, on a bare, sandy lot behind a scrubby fringe of willows. Scott had killed the siren a few blocks back, and as he pulled up at the intersection he flicked off the lights and picked up the radio mike. He glanced up at the street sign, which was legible in the bright moonlight. "This is four-oh-niner zebra," he said into the mike. "I'm on station at Shell Lane and Maple, and I've got the informant with me. D'ya, read me, Murph?"

Darcy couldn't help smiling. *So that's how Scott managed to convince his sergeant that I should be in at the kill,* she thought. *He called me an informant.* Her stomach tensed. *But that's exactly what I am,* she realized—*a psychic informant in a kidnapping case, just like the one in Mas-*

sachusetts. She sucked in her breath. Now that she was here, the whole thing seemed so real. What would Zaporra do when they closed in? Would he put up a fight? And what about Vickie? If she was in there with him, what would he do to her.

The radio crackled. "We copy, Phillips. Perkins and I are sittin' down here at the corner of Maple and Garden Lane. I'm goin' in with you." The words were spoken with a dry, Maine twang. "You ready?"

"As soon as Maxwell and Turner get here to cover," Scott said tensely. He looked up as another police car with two cops in it pulled up alongside them. One of them got out. "They're here," he reported, biting the words off. "Looks like Maxwell's going in."

"Roger," the radio said. "I'll go around the back. You and Maxwell take the front."

"Roger," Scott said, and clicked off the mike. He unsnapped his holster cover and loosened his gun. Darcy reached for the door handle.

"No, you don't," Scott gritted. "You're sitting this one out." He looked at her. "Sorry, Darcy, but those are orders. My orders." He gave her the ghost of a grin. "I want you—and I want you alive, not dead." He looked at her for a long moment.

"Lock yourself in," he ordered. Without another word, he left the car, closing the door quietly behind him.

Darcy saw his shadowy figure, doubled over, running through the willows. Instinctively, she crossed her fingers. *God, let him be safe,* she prayed, and braced herself for the sound of gunshots.

But they never came. Three minutes later, a beat-up red pickup with no lights was screeching out of the driveway, quickly, turning, and heading down Maple. Scott sprinted back to the car, turned on the ignition, and switched on the bubble on top of the car. The siren came to life with an ear-splitting wail. Beside them, the other police car was already pulling out to chase the pickup, its tires spinning.

"What is it?" Darcy cried, feeling the adrenaline surge.

"That's Zaporra in the pickup," Scott spit out. "He's making a break for it. Hang on."

The car leapt forward, and Darcy reached for something to hang on to. "Does he have Vickie with him?" she yelled over the shriek of the siren.

"Negative," Scott bit out. "She may be in the house. Maxwell's still back there, checking it out."

They sped down the road, following the

153

lights of the cop car a half-block ahead of them. The pickup, another half-block ahead, was visible in the moonlight. At the next corner, the cop-car and the pickup turned right, and Scott spun his steering wheel left.

"But they're going that way!" Darcy cried.

"We're cutting him off," Scott said, and hung right at the first cross street. Two blocks later, taking another right, Scott floored it. Four blocks, and they were pulling onto the Salt Marsh one-lane blacktop, two car lengths behind the pickup, which was running with lights now, and well ahead of the other squad car. With her feet braced against the floorboard, Darcy sneaked a glance at the speedometer. They were topping eighty. "God," she breathed.

"Don't worry," Scott said grimly. "I've had plenty of practice—on our training course."

Darcy knew that Salt Marsh Road, dead-ended at an abandoned fishing pier, a mile up ahead. Scott's car was faster than Zaporra's old rattletrack pickup, and they were rapidly gaining on him. In a half mile, Scott had closed the distance. They were on Zaporra's back bumper. Darcy could see that the body of the pickup was piled with boxes and junk. They jolted loosely as the pickup took each pothole.

Darcy twisted around in her seat. "The other squad car," she said. "It's not following us! I don't see the lights."

"Damn," Scott muttered. "Porter said he was having trouble with the fuel pump. It probably went out on him. Looks like it's just you and me, babe." He bent over the wheel. "Duck down," he commanded. "I'm going around on the left, and the guy may decide to shoot."

Without arguing, Darcy scrunched down in her seat. Scott dropped two wheels into the weedy ditch and bounced past the pickup, fighting to keep control of the car. When they had passed Zaporra, Darcy raised herself in the seat and looked back. In the moonlight, she saw that Zaporra was hunched over the steering wheel gripping it with both hands. His face was contorted with the effort of driving.

"If he's got a gun," she told Scott, "he's not holding it. It looks like it's all he can do to manage the truck."

"He's probably got the damn thing floored," Scott said grimly. He pushed their speed up more and held it until they were a good forty yards ahead of the pickup. "This is it," he said. "Brace yourself." Scott braked hard and spun the steering wheel. The squad car slewed to the right, its rear end skidding around on the gravel. It narrowly missed a 20 mph speed limit sign before it came to a bone-rattling stop, pointing down the road in the direction they had come from. Scott cut the siren.

"Geez, Scott," Darcy said into the deafening silence, "did they teach you that in cop school?"

But Scott was already out of the car, gripping his thirty-eight with both hands. Zaporra's pickup was roaring straight towards them, as if he intended to ram the car. As Darcy got her door open and tensed to jump, Scott rested his gun on the hood of the car and with one quick shot, picked off Zaporra's left tire. It blew with a loud bang. The truck lurched sharply to the left and bounced to a stop, twenty feet from the squad car. The door on the passenger side opened, and Zaporra half-jumped, half-fell out and began to run in the direction of the dunes. Darcy leaped out of the passenger seat of the car.

"Stop!" Scott called sharply, and holstered his gun. Zaporra responded by zig-zagging across the dry, brush-covered salt flats. Scott lowered his gun and charged after him, Darcy on his heels. With her strength and athletic build, she was almost as fast as Scott.

But it wasn't easy running. Underfoot, the sand was loose, covered with debris blown ashore by the last hurricane. Darcy was guessing at each step, hoping she could hold her step on the loose ground. She lifted her vision in time to see Scott lose his footing and fall to one knee. He pushed himself up and went on, limping badly, his body strained with pain. Zaporra had gotten lucky. With Scott slowed down, he was outdistancing them by ten yards and gaining, heading for the dunes. He seemed driven to greater speed by the urge to save his skin. Darcy drew in a hard, painful breath of air, gritted her teeth, and sprinted hard.

"Screw it, Darcy," Scott yelled, "We'll call for backup."

But Darcy disregarded him. She was gaining on Zaporra now, and he was making mistakes. As he came to the crest of a shrub-covered dune, he stumbled and nearly went down. As he tried to recover, Darcy closed the distance between them. She lowered her head like a tackle coming hard off the line and grabbed him around the knees. Zaporra gave a sharp yelp and went down. The force of the fall threw both of them over the top of the dune. They rolled, Darcy hanging on Zaporra for dear life. *For Vickie's life*, she thought, panting. The brush scraped her face, the sand filled her mouth, and she felt a sharp shell slice her arm. At the bottom of the dune, Zaporra crashed into a large log, chest first. The crash knocked the wind out of him, and he clutched his chest, moaning.

From the top of the dune, Scott yelled, "You okay, Darcy?" and he began to scramble down.

"Yeah," Darcy said. She spit sand out of her mouth and pulled Zaporra's arms behind his back, while trying to catch her breath. "A little winded, is all," she assessed.

Beneath her, Zaporra stirred and gurgled. She kneed him in the side, just enough to keep him from breaking loose. "Where's Vickie?" she demanded roughly.

He coughed. "I haven't got her," he managed. He rolled over on his side and looked up, his eyes filled with hatred. "You can beat me all to hell, but you won't get what you want. I haven't got her, I tell you."

Scott came skidding to the bottom of the dune, his gun at the ready. He unsnapped a set of cuffs from his belt, and tossed them to Darcy. Then he recited Zaporra's rights, rattling them off from memory.

Zaporra straightened up. "I don't need a lawyer, because I'm innocent."

Darcy wrenched his arms as she fastened the cuffs. "Don't lie to us," she yelled. "If you didn't kidnap Vickie, how come you split when the cops showed?"

He gave her a sideways glance full of anger and hatred.

"Because of my record," he said sullenly. "Because I knew the Thomas girl. I figured it was only a matter of time before the cops would be after me for it." He spat sand out of his mouth. "I was right, too."

"You sure were," Scott said grimly. He pulled Zaporra around. "Let's go."

The march back across the tide flats wasn't any easier than the chase had been. Zaporra was staggering, Scott was limping badly, and Darcy was feeling the effects of the tumble down the dunes. Her scratches smarted and her throat was raw from the sand. She was wondering about something, too. *When I picked up the bear in Vickie's bedroom, I got this really strong sense of evil. But why didn't I get the same feeling when I touched Zaporra?* She frowned. *I was practically sitting on him. Why didn't I feel anything?*

By the time they got back to the road, the third squad car had pulled up and three cops were waiting for them, playing a spotlight across the flats.

"Well, Phillips, it looks like you got him okay without us," one of them said.

Scott grinned. "She got him, Sergeant." He gestured with his head toward Darcy as he leaned Zaporra up against the pickup and began to pat him down.

The cops looked at Darcy. "*She* did?" one of them asked incredulously. "She must be one killer chick."

"You're Darcy Laken?" Sergeant Murphy said, stepping forward. "You're the one responsible for the tip?"

Darcy nodded shortly. Something was pushing at the fringes of her awareness, something—

"I've never held much with psychics," the sergeant said, raising black eyebrows. "But I have to say, you're making a believer out of—"

The sergeant's compliments faded out of Darcy's mind. Something else was trying to catch her attention. *What is it?* she questioned. *What is it?*

She turned abruptly and went to the back of the pickup. The boxes and junk were still there, strewn around in the bed.

160

One box had broken open, spilling its contents. Darcy saw a corner of something light-colored, and reached for it, pulling it out of the mess.

It was a monogrammed cardigan sweater, that looked a rich, rosy pink color in the white headlights. *VT,* the darker pink monogram said. The right sleeve, from cuff to elbow, was stained with dried blood. Darcy held the sweater, bracing herself in anticipation of the dark, smothering evil she'd sensed when she had picked up the stuffed bear.

But there was nothing. She waited. After a long moment Darcy closed her eyes and held the bloody sleeve against her face, willing herself to be open, to accept whatever messages the sweater held for her, no matter how dark and fearsome.

Again, nothing, except for the faint, old-fashioned scent of lilies of the valley lingering on the sweater.

On the other side of the truck, one of the cops said, "Get in there, you," and a door slammed. *They must be taking Zaporra to the police station for questioning and booking,* Darcy thought. *Will he tell them where Vickie is?* She looked at the sweater, frowning. *Where is Vickie?*

Scott came around the back of the truck.

161

"What are you doing back here?" he asked. His eyes were warm. "You okay, Darcy? That was one hell of a tumble you took. I have to tell you, you've really made a hit with the sergeant. And he's not easy to impress. He's—"

Darcy handed him the sweater.

He stared down at the monogram. "Vickie's?"

Darcy nodded.

Scott shook his head. "Well, I guess I don't need ESP to tell me we've got our man." His mouth clamped into a thin line. "Sorry to tell you this, Darcy, but Vickie's not in the house. Zaporra must be keeping her somewhere else."

Darcy looked down at the bloodstain. *Yes,* she thought. *We've got our man. But why didn't I feel anything when I was sitting on Zaporra? And why don't I feel anything from Vickie's sweater? It could only mean one thing—Vickie is dead.*

TEN

The questions were still echoing in Darcy's mind the next morning as she went down to the kitchen to make breakfast. *Why didn't I get a flash of some kind from Zaporra?* she kept thinking. *Or from the sweater?*

Molly came in, wearing jeans and a denim shirt embroidered with horses. "Did I hear a car door slam about midnight last night?" she asked.

"Yeah." Darcy popped two waffles into the toaster. "That was me, coming home." She poured Molly a glass of orange juice. "Scott and I got Zaporra last night."

"Got who?" Molly demanded. "What are you talking about?"

"We captured the guy who kidnapped Vickie," Darcy replied patiently, and then she told Molly what happened.

"And you let me sleep through the whole

163

thing?" Molly wailed. "There you were, out there tackling a kidnapper, and here I was—"

"Believe me," Darcy said firmly, "It wasn't much fun." She retrieved the maple syrup from the refrigerator. "Anyway, there's a problem."

"What kind of problem?" Molly demanded. "Apart from the fact that the creep didn't say where he's keeping Vickie, I mean."

Darcy sighed. "I'm just not sure what's going on now," she said. She sat down on a stool at the counter. "I got absolutely zilch from him. And when I picked up Vickie's sweater . . ." She shook her head. "Zip again."

"No flashes?"

"No flashes, no messages, no secret code, no nothing." Darcy took the waffles out of the toaster and handed one to Molly. She put the other on her plate and poured syrup over it. "If he's the kidnapper, why didn't I feel something?" She bit her lip. "And why didn't I get something from the sweater? Does it mean that there's nothing left to feel—that Vickie's dead?"

"Well, maybe," Molly said doubtfully. "But wouldn't you still feel—" The phone rang. Molly reached for it and spoke briefly before handing it to Darcy. "It's for you," she said. "Scott the Cop. Hey, get the story from him, will you? I gotta know what's going on!"

Darcy reached eagerly for the receiver. "Yeah, Scott," she said. "How'd it go with Zaporra?"

"Not so great," Scott said wearily. "We've been interrogating him all night."

"And what'd you find out?"

"Zippo." Scott sounded discouraged. "He keeps saying he didn't have anything to do with it, and we haven't been able to shake his story. But he doesn't have an alibi for the night Vickie disappeared. He says he was out fishing, but he can't name anybody to confirm."

"How does he explain Vickie's sweater in the back of his truck?"

"Says he gave her a ride home one day and she left it. He didn't return it to her because he . . . well, he said he had this crush on her. He says he knows it was dumb to keep it, but he couldn't bring himself to give it back. When he got scared that we might get on his trail, he figured he'd better get rid of it. That's why it was with the trash in the back of his truck. He was going to drop it at the dump."

Molly nudged Darcy. "What'd Scott say about the sweater?"

"He says Vickie left it in his truck," Darcy explained, "the day he gave her a lift." She frowned, her skin prickling. *Something's not right here,* she thought. *What is it?*

"And the blood?" Molly asked with another nudge. "What's his explanation for that?"

"What about the blood?" Darcy asked almost automatically. *Something's not right,* she thought again. *And it's got to do with Vickie's sweater. Why didn't I feel anything when I picked it up? It was the sweater she was wearing when she was kidnapped, wasn't it?*

"He says she had a nosebleed," Scott replied.

Darcy turned to Molly. "Nosebleed."

"Likely story," Molly muttered. She leaned close to the receiver and raised her voice so Scott could hear her. "Sounds like a lie to me."

Scott chuckled. "Sounds like it to us, too," he said. "But all we can do is keep at it until we break him. Nobody's buying his explanation, of course."

Suddenly Darcy flashed on what it was that was bothering her. *The sweater!* she realized. *It wasn't the one Vickie was wearing that day!* "Maybe you should, Scott," she said quietly. "Maybe Zaporra's telling the truth."

Molly goggled at her. "What are you talking about?!"

There was a moment's silence on the other end of the line, then Scott said, "Whoa, time out. I think I'm missing something. Isn't this the guy who was convicted of kidnapping in California? Isn't this the guy you said kidnapped Vickie?"

Darcy squirmed uncomfortably. "Well, yeah . . ." *Yeah, I said that. And I had good reason to, given the information I had. But now—*

"And now all of a sudden you're telling me that he didn't do it?"

Darcy pulled in her breath. "Do you remember what Vickie's parents said she was wearing the day she disappeared?"

"Yeah," Scott replied, "A plaid skirt, a white turtleneck, a sweater—"

"A *blue* sweater," Darcy said.

Molly leaned forward. "Hey, I thought you said it was pink. With a monogram."

"It was a pink sweater we found in Zaporra's truck last night," Darcy told her. "But the one she had on the day she disappeared was blue."

"Yeah, you're right," Scott agreed.

"I know," Darcy said. "I saw her that day, remember? I should have thought of it last night, but with all the excitement, I just didn't—"

Scott's voice was tense. "Murphy's yelling at me to get off the phone. I've gotta go. I'll check this out and get back to you later."

"Okay," Darcy said. "Maybe Molly and I will go over to Vickie's house and see if we can clear up this thing about the sweater."

"Yeah," Scott said. He paused, and his voice lightened. "But if you get a psychic flash while you're over there, do me a favor, huh? Tell me about it later, when this whole thing is over."

"We'll see, Scott. We'll see." Darcy hung up the phone and turned to Molly. "Come on," she said. "We're outta here!"

Virginia Thomas stopped pacing the floor and sank down on the sofa. "Thank God they've found this man," she said, running her hands through her blond hair. "But where is Vickie?" Her voice rose shrilly. "What has he done with her?"

"Now, honey," Clark Thomas said, reaching out to comfort his wife. "I keep telling you, over and over. It doesn't help to—"

"I know it doesn't," Mrs. Thomas cried, her shoulders shaking. "But what else can I do? I've gone out with the search parties every day. I've appeared on television and pleaded for information. Now they've captured her kidnapper and he won't tell them what he's done with her!"

Darcy could feel a heavy lump in her throat. *How would I feel if it was Patsi or Lilly who was missing? I'd be frantic, that's how. I wouldn't just go on TV or look under rocks. I'd probably be breaking heads.* She leaned forward. "There's something I need to ask you, Mrs. Thomas," she said urgently. "It's about Vickie's pink sweater."

"Her *pink* sweater?" Clark Thomas asked. He looked at his wife. "I thought she was wearing a blue sweater when she disappeared."

Mrs. Thomas sat up and blew her nose. "That's right. The blue one we gave her for her birthday. It matches her blue plaid skirt."

"I know," Darcy said. "I'm asking about a different sweater. A pink cardigan with a monogram."

Mrs. Thomas wiped her eyes. "Well *I*

169

have one like that," she said. "Except I haven't seen it in a while."

"You have one?" Darcy asked, puzzled.

Mrs. Thomas nodded. "Vickie borrowed it a few weeks ago and didn't return it. I only missed it after she—" Her mouth tightened. "Why are you asking?"

Of course, Darcy thought, *V.T. Virginia Thomas, Vickie Thomas. Vickie and her mother have the same initials.* "Because that's the sweater I found in Chuck Zaporra's truck last night," she said. "It was pink, with a VT monogram."

"That was the sweater with the blood on it," Molly explained excitedly. "Zaporra says that she left it in his truck. And the blood—"

"Came from a nosebleed," Darcy said.

"Well, that much is possible, anyway," Clark Thomas said. "Vickie is prone to nosebleeds every once in a while. Sometimes it's kind of hard to stop them."

"So," Darcy said slowly, "Zaporra could be telling the truth after all."

"Telling the truth?" Mrs. Thomas gave Darcy a dazed look. "You mean, you think he didn't kidnap Vickie?"

"I don't know what to think," Darcy said, feeling terribly confused. She stood up and took a deep breath. Last time, she'd gotten

170

into Vickie's bedroom with a trick. *This time,* she thought determinedly, *I have to do this straight.*

"Mrs. Thomas," she said, "I know this is going to sound weird, but I'd like to spend a few minutes in Vickie's bedroom. You see, sometimes I—"

"Sometimes she gets these psychic flashes," Molly broke in eagerly. "She knows things. Like, she knew about my accident, before it happened. And she knew about Chuck Zaporra. She's the one who gave his name to the police."

"But maybe I really didn't know about Zaporra," Darcy said. She held out her hands apologetically. "Maybe I've screwed things up, trusting my intuition. That's what I have to find out. Because if Zaporra didn't do it, somebody else did, and we've been wasting precious time chasing after him." Darcy looked at the Thomases.

Will they believe me? she wondered. *Or will they think I'm some sort of freak? But they did say they knew about Vickie's work with Dr. Cassidy. And Mr. Thomas even encouraged it. . . .*

Mrs. Thomas was frowning, but Mr. Thomas was leaning forward, almost eagerly. "Vickie always said she was psychic, too. Do you think you can find her?"

Darcy laughed shakily. "So far," she said, "I've pretty much struck out. But I'd like to try again, if it's all right with you."

Mrs. Thomas shook her head. "If you ask me, this is all a bunch of nonsense."

"What can it hurt, Ginny?" Mr. Thomas asked cajolingly. "All she wants to do is look around in Vickie's bedroom."

Mrs. Thomas shrugged, as if it wasn't worth arguing about. "Well, I guess."

Vickie's room looked exactly as it had a few days before, only this time Darcy wasn't alone in it. Molly was there, and Clark and Virginia Thomas were standing in the doorway watching. Mr. Thomas's face was hopeful. Mrs. Thomas's arms were folded and she looked skeptical.

Once again, Darcy made a tour of the room, touching everything, even the clothes in the closet, which still faintly smelled of Vickie's perfume. And once again, she felt nothing until she came to the innocent-looking brown plush bear on the bed. The minute she picked it up, she felt it again—the ominous, overwhelming evil, rising up and surrounding her like a black, foul-smelling fog. It permeated her mind. She closed her eyes and tried to close her mind against its pervasive power—and to open herself to Vickie.

Vickie? she thought. *Vickie, where are you?*

No answer. And she couldn't hold on to the bear any longer. She dropped it as if it were burning hot.

"Darcy?" Molly asked worriedly. "What's wrong?"

Darcy turned, forcing herself to smile. She didn't want to alarm Vickie's parents, or to let them know the true magnitude of what she had felt. "This little guy is sure cute," she said, looking down at the bear. "I'll bet he misses Vickie, too."

Mr. Thomas made a strangled sound. "Yes," he said. "That's her pet bear. She only got it a little while back, but she liked it a lot." He stopped, cleared his throat, and spoke again. "She loved her stuffed animals. She always named them, you know. That tiger—his name is Tigger, after the Winnie-the-Pooh character."

"And the bear?" Darcy asked, trying to lighten her voice and make it sound casual. "Does he have a name?"

"Cassidy," Clark Thomas said.

Darcy's heart jumped up into her throat. "Cassidy?" Her voice faltered. "Where'd she get him?"

It was Mrs. Thomas who answered. "The bear was a thank-you present from one of her professors. The one Vickie helped with the psych research." She looked at Darcy. "Maybe you know him, Darcy. Professor Cassidy. He's in the psychology department."

Darcy swallowed hard. "Yes, I know him," she said quietly. "I know Dr. Cassidy."

ELEVEN

"I think you'd better run that by me again," Molly said as Darcy pulled her van over to the edge of the road, and parked at a point overlooking the ocean. "I'm not sure I heard you right."

It sounded crazy to Darcy's own ears, but she repeated what she had said. "I think Dr. Cassidy is somehow mixed up in Vickie's kidnapping."

"Don't you know how weird that sounds?" Molly insisted. "What made you think of it?"

"It's the bear," Darcy explained. "When I picked it up, both times I got this—" She shook her head and stared out at the sea gulls circling over the rocky beach below. "It's hard to describe. It just feels like evil, that's all." Her voice choked. "Terrible, awful evil."

Molly shook her head doubtfully. "I don't

know, Darcy. Professors just don't do things like that. And you trusted him to hypnotize you. You must have thought he was ok?"

What Molly said was true—legitimate university professors doing legitimate research work didn't kidnap their students. On the other hand . . .

Darcy closed her eyes, trying to think the whole thing through. "It's more than just the name," she said. "Dr. Cassidy gave Vickie the bear. And no, I'm not saying he did it himself. Maybe he's in on it with Zaporra." She shook her head, feeling confused and uncertain. "I just wish I could remember what went on in my sessions with him," she muttered. "But I was hypnotized. I don't remember a thing."

Molly turned to face her. "Is that really true?" she asked. "You've had two whole sessions with him and you don't remember anything?"

"I remember the beginnings of the sessions," Darcy said, "before he hypnotized me. And the ends, too. But as far as the rest of it—all I know is what he told me when I woke up. The first time, he said I named Kleister, or rather Keister—" She snapped her fingers, the light suddenly beginning to dawn. "Molly, Cassidy's the one who said I named Kleister!"

Molly looked puzzled. "So?" She frowned, thinking. "So maybe—"

"So maybe I wasn't the one who came up with Zaporra's name, after all!" Darcy exclaimed. "Maybe Cassidy planted the information, figuring I'd take it straight to the police! I mean, he knew that my boyfriend is a cop. How much more convenient could it be?"

"You mean, he, like, framed Zaporra? Is that what you're saying?"

"Yeah, that's exactly what I'm saying. Somehow he found out that Zaporra's real name is Kleister, and he learned about the kidnapping conviction. It might not be hard to do. Maybe he knew Zaporra's probation officer back in California. Or he got hold of Zaporra's personnel records at the university. And maybe he knew that Zaporra had once given Vickie a ride— maybe Vickie even told Cassidy about it herself."

Molly was nodding. "So he kidnapped Vickie and then told you that you said it was Zaporra who did it!"

"And don't forget that there was another kidnapping last year," Darcy reminded her. "Marsha Grant. She was a university student—and she took a psych course! At least that's what a guy in my criminology class said. So she must have known Cassidy, too."

Molly shook her head dubiously. "I don't know, Darcy. Didn't you tell me that the guy is a world-class researcher? I mean, he's got to be pretty important, right?"

"All we know," Darcy said, "is what Cassidy and Frieda have told us. Maybe Cassidy isn't such an expert after all. I wonder how long he's been at the university?"

"Yes, but still," Molly said. "Do you honestly believe that he could have forced two girls to—"

Darcy's breath caught in her throat. "He wouldn't have to force them," she said. "Not if he hypnotized them, the way he hypnotized me. Under hypnosis, they'd do exactly what he wanted. And they'd do it afterward, too. With the right post-hypnotic suggestion, all he had to do was make a date with them and they'd go away with him." Her blood ran cold. *And never come back.*

Molly's frown had deepened. "Yes, but I've always heard that if somebody's hyp-notized, they'll only do what they think is right. How could he convince them to do something they didn't really want to do?"

"I don't know," Darcy said. "That's something I'll have to find out." She turned on the ignition and jammed the van into gear.

"Where are we going?" Molly asked.

"To the cop shop," Darcy said. Though Scott had told her not to call him with her psychic flashes until after this was over, this was one flash she couldn't ignore. Scott Phillips was going to have to listen to what she had to say. If Cassidy was involved in this, maybe he could lead them to Vickie!

Scott shook his head. He, Darcy, and Molly were in the break room, sitting over coffee. It had only taken a few minutes for Darcy to tell Scott what she'd come up with.

He shook his head. "Look," he said, "you led us to Kleister and the bloody sweater, so I know you're onto something, Darcy. And I admit that we've run into a dead end with Zaporra. Looks like we've got all we're going to get out of him. But this—" He stood up and tossed his empty paper cup in the waste basket. "I mean, you're talking about a highly respected university professor. If you're wrong, it could mean trouble for everybody—big time."

"Wait, Scott," Molly protested. "Sit down. You're not taking this seriously enough."

"I am taking it seriously," Scott said. "I am seriously thinking of what could happen if we picked up Cassidy on your say-so, without any evidence, and he sued us for false arrest."

Darcy stood up, too. "Okay," she said with a sigh, "if evidence is what you need, I'll get you evidence."

He eyed her thoughtfully. "What kind of evidence are we talking about?"

"I don't know what Cassidy's game is," she said, "but it's my guess that he's in this up to his neck. If he didn't take Vickie himself, he knows who did. Plus, he knows where she is. Scott, I hope you believe me, but if you don't, I'm finding out what I can on my own."

"You don't have to go alone, Darcy," Molly said firmly. "I'm in it with you. I don't know about this Cassidy guy, but I trust your intuition. I think you're on the right track."

Scott gave Darcy a narrow look. "And just what is it you're thinking of doing to trap this master criminal, Sherlock Holmes?"

"Very funny," Molly muttered, shaking her head.

"I've got an appointment with Cassidy in the morning," Darcy told Scott. "He's going to hypnotize me again. But this time, I'll be carrying a *working* tape recorder in my purse. Or maybe in my pocket, with the mike under my blouse. And this time, I'm not going to let him—"

Molly's mouth dropped open. "Your blouse?" she said. "Darcy, do you remember about the button?"

Darcy frowned. "What button?"

"Didn't you lose a button the day that you had your last session with this guy? Do you suppose—"

Darcy's eyes widened. "You mean, he—" She closed her eyes. She could feel her face flaming red. "Oh God," she whispered.

Scott looked from one of them to the other. "If it's not too much trouble," he said dryly, "would you two mind telling me what you're talking about?"

"We're talking about molestation," Molly shot back. "Sexual assault. That's what we're talking about! This guy hypnotizes girls, and while they're lying there, powerless, he—" She turned to gag. "Excuse me while I throw up."

Darcy turned to Scott. "When I got home

181

Monday night, the button on my blouse was missing. Maybe it isn't solid proof, but it's one more indication that Cassidy's up to something. I'm going to find out what it is. So tomorrow I'm—"

"Whoa," Scott cautioned, holding up both hands. "If this guy is really involved in this thing, I can't let you—"

"If this guy is really involved," Molly said sweetly, "you'll wire her."

Scott looked at her. "Forget that," he snapped. "Murph would never in a zillion years let me use a civilian to do a—"

"Hey, wait, Scott," Darcy said. "If I'm right, this man has kidnapped and maybe murdered two girls—and molested God knows how many. I've got an inside track. I'm going to see him tomorrow, and I think I can trick him into revealing the truth. Are you going to let this chance go to waste?"

"Waste?" Scott put his hands on her shoulders, his eyes intent, his voice rough. "If you're right, Darcy, this guy is planning to waste you! Do you think I'd let you run that kind of risk?"

Darcy pulled back, staring at Scott. *Of course!* she thought. *That's what Frieda was flashing on when she said I was in danger! She's psychic, too. She saw that I'm*

182

next on Cassidy's hit list—although she probably didn't realize it had anything to do with her beloved doctor! Molly wheeled her chair in between Darcy and Scott. "Hey, time out, you guys," she said. "We're not going to get anywhere by nuking each other. Hold your fire for the enemy."

Scott sat down on the sofa. Numbly, Darcy sank down beside him, still trying to get a grasp on what this all meant.

"That's better," Molly said. "Look, Scott, if you don't let Darcy go in, what're your alternatives?"

"We can put somebody in there undercover," Scott said. "A policewoman who's trained for this sort of—"

"And just how long will that take?" Darcy demanded. "God, Scott, if we're right, Cassidy's been holding Vickie for eight days. How much longer can she last? Can we afford to hang around and twiddle our thumbs while you plant somebody— somebody who's psychic enough to pass his ESP test—in his lab?"

"Especially," Molly pointed out, "when you've got Darcy already. All you have to do is put a bug on her and—"

Scott groaned. "You guys are talking like I could do this on my own hook. Forget that. Murphy would have my badge. And he'd never give me the go-ahead. Not for something as risky as this."

"Yes, he would," Darcy said quietly. "But he won't unless you tell him that I'm volunteering." She looked at Scott squarely. "Unless you remind him that I'm the one who chased Zaporra down and that I can handle myself in a tough situation. And unless you tell him that it's probably the only way to get to Vickie—if she's still alive."

Scott looked at Darcy for a long moment. Finally he nodded. "Yeah. Well, when you put it like that—"

"Thanks, Scott," Darcy said softly. "I knew I could count on you."

"So what's the deal, Scott?" Molly asked later that evening, when he arrived at the Mason's. "What are we going to do?"

"The deal," Scott said, "is that Darcy goes in with a wire."

"Great!" Molly exclaimed. "That's terrific."

"Thanks, Scott," Darcy said. But although she felt relieved, she felt apprehensive, too. It was dangerous. *Can I pull it off?* she wondered. *How can I get him to say anything incriminating enough to convince the cops to pick him up for questioning?*

*And what if he somehow figures out what
I'm up to? What will he do?*

"There's more," Scott said. "I'm going in,
too. I'll be there with you."

"With me?" Darcy said, alarmed. "Hey,
no way! I'd be safe, but Cassidy won't try
anything if you're sitting there holding my
hand!"

Scott grinned. "Don't sweat it, Darcy.
We've already set it up with the university's security people. They're going to give
us an assist on this. So while you're in with
Cassidy, I'll be across the hall, listening to
every word."

"And I'll be parked outside in the van,"
Molly said excitedly. "In case he tries to get
away. That way we'll have all bases covered."

"More than you know," Scott replied.
"We'll have three or four plainclothes university security people in the building and
outside, just to make sure the guy doesn't
make a break for it."

Darcy frowned. *It's great to know that
Scott wants to protect me,* she thought, *but
maybe it won't work.* "It sounds like a cast
of thousands, Scott. But what if Cassidy
sees all these people hanging around and
gets suspicious? Maybe I'd just better do it
alone."

185

Scott put both hands on her shoulders. "If you think for a minute I'd let you go in with that nut-case without any backup," he said firmly, "you're as wacky as he is. Now we'd better all catch a few zzz's. Tomorrow's gonna be a real busy day."

It took Darcy a long time to fall asleep that night. She kept thinking nervously about what might happen the next day, and whether she'd be able to fool Cassidy into thinking she was only pretending to be hypnotized. But most of all, she was thinking about Vickie. Would they ever find her? Or would they find her when it was too late?

As Darcy started to go into the lab reception room the next day, she noticed that the doorway to the office across the hall was slightly ajar. With a quick glance over her shoulder to make sure the hallway was empty, she stepped through the door. Scott was bent over a book at a desk in the corner, as if he were a graduate student, studying. He was wearing street clothes and a fanny pack, and something was tucked into one ear, like a tiny hearing aid. *It's the receiver,* she thought. *And that thing he's wearing on his belt must be the recorder pack.*

"Hi," she said.

He turned around. "Hi." His smile was crooked and there was a line from worry between his eyes. "All set?"

"All set," Darcy said, trying to be casual. "Wish me luck."

"You got it, Darcy," he said softly. "Watch yourself."

Across the hall, Frieda was at her desk, as usual. "Hello, Darcy," she said. But her voice lacked its usual cheerfulness, and her eyes held a worried look. "Dr. Cassidy's waiting for you."

Darcy wanted to ask her whether she was getting some kind of flash, but she stopped herself. *If she is, it won't help me to know about it,* she thought. *And if she isn't, that might mean I'm wrong. Either way, I'll know soon enough.* "Okay," was all she said.

As she went down the hall, Darcy touched the ladybug pin on her blouse. It was cute, although not something she'd normally buy for herself. *Nobody would ever guess that this bug is really a bug,* she thought, with a half-smile. Then she shivered. *But what if Dr. Cassidy guesses? What will he do?* Suddenly she was grateful to have Scott—solid, dependable, caring Scott—sitting across the hall from her, listening to every word.

"I'm going in, Scott," she whispered to the ladybug. "Stay tuned."

Dr. Cassidy was waiting for her, the office lights already turned low. "Darcy," he said, "I thought we'd get right to work." He locked the door.

Darcy almost panicked. *He can't lock the door!* she thought. *If Scott needs to get in here, he won't be able to!* "How about some music?" she asked. "Last time, it really helped."

"Sure," Dr. Cassidy said. She waited until he was bending over the stereo, then she surreptitiously unlocked the door.

Dr. Cassidy turned around unaware. "Are we ready?" he asked, smiling.

"I guess," Darcy said, trying not to show how apprehensive she felt. She tossed her dark hair and moved to the sofa. "What about the tape recorder?" she asked. "Did you get it fixed?"

"Not yet," Dr. Cassidy said regretfully. "But I promise to take good notes. Now just lie down—okay?"

Both times before, Darcy had been willing to be hypnotized, not because hypnosis was fun, but because she'd really wanted to find out about Vickie. Now, being hypnotized was the last thing in the world she wanted. She was counting on her strong will to keep her from going under—her will, and her fear about what might happen if she did.

But can I resist? she wondered anxiously, as she lay down. *Will I be able to keep from—*

"Just relax," Dr. Cassidy instructed, smiling. The dimple flashed in his cheek. "You remember how easy this is, don't you, Darcy? I know you want to help Vickie. Your eyes are getting heavy, your breathing is slowing . . ."

Darcy closed her eyes and let her muscles go limp and her breathing slow, playing the part of an obedient subject. But she refused to let go of her consciousness. What did this guy think he was doing, luring young women in here and using them for his own purposes? Who did he think he was, getting them to trust him and then betraying them? And with the questions came another feeling, an intense, fiery anger.

To hell with you, mister, she thought fiercely. *You're not going to sweet-talk me, the way you did Vickie and Marsha. I won't be so easy to con.*

". . . deep in trance," Dr. Cassidy's deep, rich voice crooned. He was leaning closer, very close. Darcy could feel his breath on her face, his hand on her arm. *This is just like before,* she realized hotly, *but I was too far out of it to know what he was doing!*

He stroked Darcy's hair as she lay still, pretending to be hypnotized. "Such a pretty, pretty girl," he crooned. "So much prettier than—" He stopped, his breath coming heavier. "Oh, yes, Darcy Laken, I'm going to be very good to you." He brushed her cheek with his lips, touched her eyes, her forehead. "Just relax. I won't hurt you. I'll take care of you the same way Scott takes care of you."

At the sound of Scott's name, Darcy involuntarily stiffened. *Scott? What was he doing using Scott's name?*

"That's okay, Darcy," Dr. Cassidy said soothingly. "Just pretend I'm your boy-friend. I'm Scott." His voice dropped lower. "Scott is touching your hair, your lips."

Woozily, Darcy felt Dr. Cassidy's fingers. *So that was the cheap trick he used to get his subjects to let him do whatever he wanted. He played on their feelings about their boyfriends—or their ex-boyfriends, in Vickie's case! He pretended to be somebody they cared for, in order to get them to let him touch them!*

I can't let him get to me! Darcy admonished herself. But she'd given in before, unwittingly, and it was getting awfully hard to hold back now. Try as she might, she was fading into the blackness. She was losing it. "Scott," she murmured, hoping blurrily that the bug was picking up her voice. "Scott, where are you? I need you, Scott."

"Scott is here with you now," Dr. Cassidy whispered close to her ear. "You do need him. You need him more than you've ever needed him before. And he's going to satisfy you, totally satisfy you." Darcy felt lips pressing hers and heard a soft whisper. "Scott is kissing you, Darcy. You like it when Scott kisses you, don't you?"

"Yes," Darcy murmured, her insides going soft. "I want him to kiss me. . . ." Half-hypnotized, the line between reality and fantasy was blurring. Had Scott come to rescue her? Was he here, holding her? "Yes, I do like it." She felt her arms going around his neck, felt herself pressing against him, a new kind of excitement flooding through her like a warm soft wave, dissolving all her resistance. "Kiss me again, Scott," she whispered. "Please don't stop kissing me."

"I won't," Dr. Cassidy said tenderly. He caressed her throat. "I'll never stop kissing you, Darcy. You're mine, mine forever." He paused, his hand dropping lower, fumbling with her buttons.

Darcy tensed in his arms, the spell suddenly broken. *Scott's never tried to undress me!* she thought, horrified.

Suddenly she heard a crash, followed by Scott's voice, loud and harsh. "Snap her out of it, you scum bag! And do it now!"

Dr. Cassidy stood up. "What is the meaning of this?" he demanded angrily, hands on hips. "What are you doing, breaking into my office and—"

"Dr. Cassidy!" It was Frieda's voice. She sounded frantic. "I tried to stop this man, but he—"

"You're under arrest for sexual assault," Scott yelled.

"No!" Frieda screamed.

Darcy opened her eyes and struggled to sit up. "It's okay, Scott," she said dizzily. Her face began to burn, as she remembered what she'd said. *Did he hear it—all of it?*

"Dr. Cassidy—" Frieda cried.

"Just a minute," Dr. Cassidy said. "I don't know what this is about, young man, but you've interrupted a very delicate process. If I don't bring this young woman out of her hypnotic trance correctly, there could be lasting consequences."

"Then do it, damn it!" Scott shouted. Darcy saw that he was holding his gun. "Get on with it!"

Frieda moaned.

Dr. Cassidy bent over Darcy. "You're waking up now, Darcy," he said. "On the count of three, you'll be fully awake and alert. One, two, three."

Darcy sat up and Scott rushed over to her, holding his gun.

"Are you okay?" he asked roughly. "That guy didn't—"

Darcy shook her head. "I'm fine," she said, her cheeks flaming. She stood up. "I hope you don't think I—I didn't mean to—"

At that moment, Dr. Cassidy grabbed Frieda and pulled her in front of him. "I'm getting out of here," he yelled. "And don't try to stop me!" Dragging Frieda with him as a shield, he made for the door. With a shout, Scott was on his heels, Darcy right behind him.

When they got to the reception room, Frieda was crumpled on the floor. Scott raced out after Cassidy, while Darcy bent over Frieda, who struggled to sit up.

"What's going on?" she cried hysterically. "Why's that man chasing Dr. Cassidy with a gun? We've got to call the police!"

193

Darcy pulled her up. "He is the police," she said.

"Then why did Dr. Cassidy run?" Frieda cried, tears welling up in her eyes.

Darcy looked at her. "You don't want to know, Frieda," she said. *But maybe, unconsciously,* she thought, *she already knows. He was probably doing the same thing to her, and giving her post-hypnotic suggestions to forget what happened between them—to trust him, no matter what.* "You'd better stay put," Darcy added sympathetically. "The police will want to talk to you. And hang onto the sign-in sheet. I've got a feeling they'll need to see it."

By the time Darcy ran into the hallway, it was empty. She sprinted for the door to the alley, where Molly was parked. She pushed the door open and ran outside, just in time to catch the last of the action.

Dr. Cassidy was running down the narrow alley with Molly gunning the van at his heels. Scott was running beside the van. The alley came to a dead end against the basement entrance to the Chemistry Building, where Dr. Cassidy was headed. He jerked frantically at the doors, but they were locked. Over them, Darcy saw a sign that read "Use Maple Street Entrance."

Dr. Cassidy whirled, his eyes darting

wildly from side to side, searching for an escape. But there was none. He was backed up against the locked doors and Scott and the van were coming at him. Molly slammed on the brakes inches from his knees, pinning him in the doorway entrance. He was trapped.

Scott stepped around the van. "Put your hands up," he snapped, "Don't move."

A plainclothesman moved up behind Scott. Molly put the van into reverse and backed up a few feet. A stocky, middle-aged campus cop jogged past Darcy, barking commands into a walkie-talkie. A couple of students stood by curiously watching.

Dr. Cassidy raised his hands. Scott pulled the handcuffs off his belt, yanked Dr. Cassidy's hands behind him, and cuffed him. "Here's your man, Jenkins," he said to the campus security officer. He touched the recorder pack he was wearing. "We've got all the evidence we need to make a sexual assault charge stick—and stick tight."

Jenkins nodded. "Good work, Phillips," he said grimly. "Come on," he said to Dr. Cassidy. "We're going to campus security to listen to a tape."

Behind her, Darcy heard the wail of a

siren. A gray university squad car pulled up and the doors opened. With the campus cop pulling one arm and Scott the other, Cassidy stumbled back up the alley. As he passed Darcy, his head jerked up.

"You," he muttered, baring his teeth. "I knew you weren't the right type for my research. I never should have taken you on."

"You're right," Darcy said. She could feel the adrenaline pumping in her veins and her heart pounding. "You never should have taken me on." She stepped forward, her hands balled into tight fists, as the campus cop opened the squad door and got ready to push Cassidy in. "Where's Vickie Thomas?" she challenged.

Cassidy turned and stared at her, his blue eyes cold, his handsome face unmoving.

"Vickie Thomas?" he growled. "How the hell should I know?"

TWELVE

Darcy spent the next several hours at the campus security office making a statement and answering questions about what had happened in Dr. Cassidy's office and what she suspected about Vickie.

She was surprised when they even wanted to know about her flashes of ESP. Apparently, Professor Cassidy *did* have a reputation on campus. *Too bad he wasted it all,* she thought. *He might have actually been onto something.*

Finally, half-way through the afternoon, Scott came into the waiting room where she had been told to sit and wait.

"Where's Molly?" he asked, looking around.

"She went to the swim center for therapy," Darcy said.

"I hope she's getting a better deal than we are," Scott said with a weary sigh.

"They're giving Cassidy a rough time in there, but he's not saying anything about Vickie." Scott put some papers and a pen on the table in front of Darcy. "Here's your typed statement, Darcy. Read it before you sign it, please. If you see anything that needs to be changed, now's the time to say so."

Quickly, Darcy read through her statement. "It looks okay to me," she said. She picked up the pen and signed it. "Cassidy's still holding out? How long can he play that game?"

"He's got a good defense lawyer," Scott said. "Campus security's working on him, but the whole thing's touchy. Thanks to you, we've got him on sexual assault. It's all there on the tape, every smarmy syllable. I figure he's going to plead on that one, and hope to get off with probation. But there's nothing on the tape to implicate him where Vickie and Marsha are concerned. If he refuses to talk, we haven't got anything concrete to go on. Unless we can break him or dig up some new evidence—"

"What about his house?" Darcy interrupted. "Have you looked there? Maybe he's hiding her—"

"That's our next stop," Scott said. He stood up. "But I can't go into his house without a warrant. And that requires what the law calls 'probable cause.' If Cassidy had said something about Vickie on the tape or during questioning, it would have been easier. But we had to bring Frieda in and get her to tell us that Vickie and Marsha both were the professor's research subjects. Her statement was enough to convince the judge to issue a search warrant."

"So now you've got it?" Darcy asked.

Scott nodded. "I'm on my way to Cassidy's now," he said.

Darcy reached for her jacket. "I'm coming with you," she said. "No way am I sitting this one out."

Scott's eyes twinkled. "Who says you have to?" he asked.

Dr. Cassidy lived in an upscale condo near a large patch of woods on Sunset Island. "He lives alone," Scott said as he and Darcy pulled up in front, "so there shouldn't be anybody here."

"Except for Vickie," Darcy said hopefully. She huddled into her coat as they went up the walk. It was even colder now, and starting to snow. *I hope Vickie's in there,* Darcy thought, looking up at the blank windows whose blinds were pulled.

If she is, at least she's warm. Darcy shivered, not wanting to think of the other side of the question. *If she isn't in there, where is she?*

Scott banged on the door, but there was no answer. Using the professor's key, he opened it. But the minute she stepped into the hall, Darcy knew the house was empty. "Vickie isn't here," she told Scott.

"We'll search anyway," Scott said. "The warrant allows me to look for notes he might have made on his so-called research, pictures he might have taken, that sort of thing." He took a pair of thin latex gloves out of his pocket and began to pull them on. "You can come with me, but don't touch anything. The print team will be here in a little while."

Darcy looked at Scott's gloves. "How about letting me have a pair of those?" she asked. "That way I'll be sure not to leave prints on anything." He tossed her a pair, and started down the hall.

Darcy followed Scott, pulling on her gloves. The condo was almost new. The downstairs rooms—living room, dining room, kitchen, bath—were all expensively decorated in cool monocromatic colors, but without a single personal touch. *It's almost,* Darcy thought, *as if this were a luxury hotel suite. There's nothing to show that a real person lives here.* The kitchen looked as though nobody had ever cooked a meal in it, and even the garbage was empty, clean and bare of the usual junk.

Upstairs, it was the same thing. Master bedroom and bath—beautifully decorated, neat, but impersonally chilly. The last room upstairs was Dr. Cassidy's study. Even here, everything was orderly. The papers were stacked neatly, the books stood on the shelves with their spines in a careful row, the items in the desk drawers were organized in little trays. Darcy stood in the center of the room, while Scott opened the drawers and looked through Dr. Cassidy's papers. As she stood there, she began to have a strange sense, as if there was something . . . something . . .

She closed her eyes and concentrated, trying to catch whatever it was. *Vickie?* she thought. *Vickie, is that you?*

Nothing. Not a word, not a sound, except for Scott's frustrated muttering.

Darcy opened her eyes and turned. Without knowing why, she felt herself drawn to a mirror that hung over a polished wooden table. It was a round mirror, framed in ebony, with small gilt curlicues around the edges. For an instant she thought of Tia's scrying mirror and the Ouija letters she had seen reflected in it—VT DANGER. Her skin prickled. *Is there something special about this mirror?* she wondered, staring at it. *Am I supposed to look into it, the way I looked into Tia's mirror? Or do I go through it, like Alice? Or—*

Without consciously willing it, Darcy put her gloved hand to the mirror frame and lightly touched it, pressing each gold curlique, until when she pressed, one went in, like a button, and the mirror frame swung out. She gasped and stepped back.

Scott whirled around. He was at her side in two large steps. "I looked at that mirror a couple of times and never figured it was a safe," he said. "How the hell did you know?"

Darcy managed a shaky laugh. "What do you think I've got ESP for?" she asked. "It's beginning to look like mirrors are my specialty."

Scott chuckled. "Well, now that you've found it, let's see if our friend keeps anything important in it." He reached his gloved hands inside and pulled out a box. On top were several snapshots.

"Pictures!" Darcy exclaimed.

"Yeah," Scott said grimly, laying them

out on the table. "And what pictures! This could be our case right here, even if we don't find anything else to link him to those girls."

There were a half-dozen photos, obviously taken with a Polaroid camera. Each photo showed a girl lying on the sofa in Dr. Cassidy's office at the university, her eyes closed, her hair tousled, blouse partially unbuttoned, skirt askew. Two of the pictures were of Vickie, two were of a dark-haired girl Darcy didn't know, and two were of—

"That's me!" Darcy cried, horrified. "He took a picture of me when I was hypnotized, right after he—" Her stomach heaved.

Scott shook his head. "Thank God we've got the guy under wraps." He looked down at the photos. "That one," he said, pointing to the dark-haired girl Darcy didn't know. She was petite, and very pretty, with a round little-girl face and long dark lashes. "That's Marsha Grant."

"Oh, God," Darcy breathed, feeling suddenly cold. She closed her eyes, shivering so hard that her teeth clicked. *She's dead. I know it.* "He killed her, Scott!"

"I was afraid of that," Scott said. He put his arm around her and held her close. "It looks like the professor had plans for you too, Darcy. You were going to be victim number three." Scott went back to the box, pulling out a leather-covered book. "Hey, what's this?"

"It looks like a journal," Darcy said excitedly. "One of those five-year diaries."

At that moment, Scott's beeper made a shrill sound. "Here," he said, holding out the journal, "why don't you read through this while I call the dispatcher and see what's up. You know the guy. You might catch something I'd miss."

Darcy took the journal to a chair and sat down while Scott went to the phone and called the station. She opened the leather-bound book and began to skim through it. Most of the entries were brief and not very interesting. "Submitted the article on hypnosis," was the entry for March 1. "Dropped suits off at the cleaners. Rain."

But when Darcy reached the month of Marsha Grant's disappearance, she found something a lot more chilling. "Located MG today, an excellent subject," she read. She sat up straight, her eyes glued to the page. "Early indications are that she's particularly suggestible and should respond well to hypnosis and post-hypnotic suggestion." Two days later: "Second session with

MG. Results very promising. Am developing a technique that virtually guarantees success—using the name of Marsha's boyfriend to gain her cooperation."

Darcy flushed red, remembering Dr. Cassidy's fingers fumbling at her blouse, and quickly turned another page. In the middle of the next week, he had written, "Tested post-hypnotic suggestion with MG. Experiment on Friday night. Will she come with me willingly, thinking I'm her boyfriend, or will she resist?"

Hurriedly, Darcy flipped to Saturday. It was blank, as was Sunday. Cassidy must have been too busy to write. In Monday's space, he had jotted, "MG experiment a total success. Jubilant! But what to do with her? Post-hypnotic suggestion might erase her memories, but I can't chance it." The rest of the week was filled with inconsequential notes, then, "MG problem solved."

Darcy swallowed down a feeling of nausea. Cassidy's cryptic note confirmed what she already knew—that Marsha was dead. *But what about Vickie?* she thought frantically. *Has that problem been solved too?*

Her fingers cold as ice, she skimmed through the next several months of entries until she came across the first mention of

Vickie. "VT coming in tomorrow. Blond, very pretty, possibly another MG." Then, the next day, "VT's perfect! Even better than MG—younger, more pliant, more suggestible." The following journal entries were almost the same as those for Marsha, each detailing the hypnotic sessions, the technique, the results. As Darcy read, her sick horror gradually changed to angry disgust. *What a bizarro!* she thought. *This psycho needs to be locked up forever for what he's done!*

And then she found the entry that described her. "Met DL today. An interesting challenge. Not highly suggestible, unfortunately, but even more beautiful and with extraordinary clairvoyant abilities. A compelling personality." Darcy gave a short, hard laugh. *Yeah, and what was he planning on doing with my compelling personality!*

The next entry came after the second session. "May have to take care of VT sooner than I planned, to make room for DL. She's resistant, but well worth the trouble. I can't get her out of my mind. Next session, will give her a post-hypnotic suggestion to meet "Scott" in the mall parking lot on Friday. Then she'll be mine!

This one, I might decide to keep a while longer."

Darcy dropped the journal as if it were on fire. *Would I have gone with him?* she asked herself, shaken. *No, of course not, not if I were in my right mind. But what if I thought I was going to meet Scott? What if I—*

"Find anything we can use in court?" Scott asked, coming up behind her.

Darcy jumped up. "It's all in here, Scott! Every rotten, scummy detail. How he hypnotized girls and got them to do what he wanted, by pretending to be their boyfriends. How he kidnapped Marsha and Vickie and then—"

She stopped, shaking, and Scott pulled her close. "It's okay, Darcy," he said softly, into her hair. "You're safe, and he's where he can't hurt you."

Darcy pushed his arms away. "But what about Vickie?" she cried, her heart thudding against her ribs. "Where is she? What's he done with her?" *She* can't *be dead,* she thought. *I'd know if she was dead!*

Scott bent over and picked up Dr. Cassidy's journal. As he did, another photograph fell out. Scott glanced at it, then handed it to Darcy without a word.

It was a photograph of Vickie, stripped naked, her pale skin dead-white in the impersonal glare of the camera strobe. Eyes closed, blond hair matted, she was lying on what looked like a camp cot in a dark room.

"Oh, God," Darcy breathed. And then, as she held the photo in her trembling hand, she seemed to hear Vickie's voice calling. The sound came from somewhere outside. "Scott!" she cried. "I hear her!"

"What?" Scott asked, bewildered. "Who? Vickie?"

"Yeah!" Shoving the photo in her pocket, Darcy dashed for the door. "Come on! We've got to find her!"

Outside, the snow was coming down in fat white flakes, veiling the fringe of trees along the road. It was late afternoon, and the dark twilight seemed draped over the island like a shroud. For a moment Darcy stood listening. What she heard was coming from inside her head, but she instinctively turned towards the woods behind the condo.

"This way!" she shouted and took off.

It wasn't hard to run across the short grass of the meadow, but once she had plunged into the woods, the going was much more difficult. The trees were clumped thickly together, and there were deadfalls everywhere. At one point Darcy tripped and banged her knee on a rock, and at another she thumped her forehead against a low branch and fell again. But both times she pushed herself up and kept going.

"I hope you know what you're doing," Scott panted, close behind her. "There's no way that guy could have dragged somebody through this crap. There's not even a path."

"There's a road up ahead," Darcy heard herself saying, and suddenly, there it was, with the faint print of tires still faintly visible through the accumulating snow.

"Somebody's driven down here not too long ago," Scott said, bending over to look. He straightened up. "You're on to something, Darcy. Which way do we go?"

Without hesitating, Darcy turned to the right and began to jog up the road. After fifty yards, the land dead-ended in a silent clearing. Darcy stopped and looked around.

"This is where it's coming from," she said, panting. The frigid air burned like fire in her lungs. "The signal or whatever I'm getting. But there's nothing here!"

The clearing was flat except for a

shrubby mound in one corner—and empty. There were only bushes and small trees planted in a square, as if they had once grown around a house.

"Somebody probably lived here once," Scott said. He kicked at a charred timber. "But the house must have burnt down." He threw Darcy a doubtful look. "If she's here, where is she?"

"Vickie?" Darcy cried, "Vickie, where are you?"

There was nothing but the nervous chatter of a squirrel. Scott turned, his shoulders hunched. "It doesn't look like she's here, Darcy," he said in a disappointed voice. "We'll come back later with—"

Darcy held up her hand. "Wait," she whispered. "Vickie's here! Give me a minute to look around."

She turned to pace through the clearing. And then, as she passed a clump of bushes growing on the little mound, she realized what she was seeing.

"It's a cellar, Scott!" she exclaimed. She ran around the other side of the hill. "And here's the door!"

It was a wooden door set into the ground—a new wooden door, Darcy noted—with a metal ring and a lock fastened to it. Scott picked the lock, then pulled on the ring and the door came up, revealing dark, damp stone steps.

"I'll go first," Scott said, taking a small torch out of his pocket. Darcy didn't argue.

At the foot of the steps, they paused. "Vickie?" Darcy said in a loud whisper. "Vickie, are you here?"

She was answered by a low moan.

Scott's torch shone on a camp cot. Vickie was lying on it, covered with blankets. She was deathly pale and shivering with cold, but alive.

"Vickie!" Darcy cried, and knelt down by the cot. "Are you okay?"

Vickie managed a wan smile. "Thank God," she said between parched lips. Then her eyes closed again.

Scott was half-way up the steps. "Stay with her," he commanded. "I'll get an ambulance."

Darcy nodded and reached for Vickie's hand. "You're safe now, Vickie," she said softly.

THIRTEEN

"So," Molly said, looking into the blazing fire in the Mason's family room fireplace, "Cassidy confessed the whole thing, including his attempt to frame Zaporra for Vickie's kidnapping."

"And Zaporra's free," Darcy said quietly. *But could he be free—ever—from the terrible feeling of being falsely accused?* "I'm glad," she added. "I've been feeling pretty awful, knowing I was the one who put Scott onto him."

"Yeah, maybe," Tia said. "But Cassidy was the one who made up all that stuff you were supposed to have said. About Zaporra, I mean."

"But it was true," Kenny objected. "The way I heard it, he got it all out of Zaporra's personnel record."

Darcy nodded. "Yes, but he gave it to me, knowing that my boyfriend was a cop and that I'd tell him," she said unhappily. "Me and my ESP—I played right into his hands."

"If it hadn't been for your ESP," Tia pointed out, "Vickie might never have been found. You were the one who located her—remember?"

"Yeah, I guess," Darcy said. She shook her head. "You know, it's ironic. What we thought was evidence leading to the culprit—Vickie's sweater and my button—turned out not to be significant after all. At least, not in the way we thought."

"Oh, yeah?" Tia asked, stretching out on her back before the fire. "How's that?"

"Vickie really did leave her sweater—her mother's sweater—in Zaporra's truck the day he gave her a ride," Darcy said. "She missed it, but she thought she'd left it on the ferry. Cassidy didn't know anything at all about the sweater. And my lost button wasn't his fault either."

Molly turned to her in surprise. "How do you know?"

"Because I found it on the floor of my car," Darcy said. "But it gave us an idea about what Cassidy was doing, so I guess it was still important."

Scott laughed, coming into the room with another bowl of popcorn. "That's the way police work is, Darcy. The evidence doesn't always take you where you think you're going."

Kenny reached into the cooler of soft drinks beside the couch. "This Frieda that you were talking about," he said to Darcy. "Cassidy's assistant. You said that she had been one of his research subjects, too, and that she'd had a crush on him. How come he didn't do to her what he did to the other two?"

"I guess because he needed her help to run the lab," Darcy said with a shrug. "And maybe she wasn't pretty enough for him."

"What'll happen to Cassidy now?" Tia asked.

Scott sat down beside Darcy and pulled her close to him. The fire flickered shadows across his face. "Because of the confession, Cassidy's lawyer had him plead guilty. He'll get life. Without parole."

"Wow, life," Tia said shakily. "To think of being locked up behind bars, every single day for the rest of your existence . . . I can't imagine it."

Kenny popped a Coke can. "You know," he said in a thoughtful voice, "I really can't figure the guy. He was at the start of his career, young, good-looking—"

"Yeah," Molly said. She stuck a marshmallow on a stick and held it over the flames. "Too bad he had to turn out to be such a lowlife. What a waste."

"That's what I don't understand," Kenny said, sipping his Coke. "How come a guy like that has to resort to hypnotizing women to get what he wants?"

Scott shrugged. "People have all kinds of hang-ups. This guy was apparently pretty insecure, both about women and about his work. He'd only been at the university a couple of years. His research was legitimate, although he certainly wasn't as 'world-famous' as Frieda and the others thought. But it unfortunately gave him a chance to be alone with young women he had power over. For him, the women and the power were a deadly combination."

"I guess the big question," Molly said, "is what's going to happen to Vickie."

"Yeah." Tia's voice was subdued. "It must have been totally awful, being shut up in that cellar for over a week, with him coming in every night and . . ." She closed her eyes. "God," she whispered. "I can't even think about what he did to her. Vickie couldn't even talk about it!"

There was a long silence in the room. The heat from the fire warmed her arms, but Darcy shivered. *Poor Vickie*. Cassidy

216

had admitted to raping her, and the doctors had confirmed it. *How can something that's supposed to be so wonderful be used as a weapon?* she thought. *Will Vickie ever be all right? It's been hard enough for me to deal with what he might have done to me . . .* she thought.

Tia sat up. "She called me, you know," she said. "Vickie, I mean. Yesterday afternoon, just before she and her mother left the island."

"How was she?" Kenny asked quietly.

"How would you be," Molly countered, "if something like that happened to you?"

"I think she'll be all right," Tia said. "Eventually, anyway. Her mom's taking her to Florida, for some R and R. And when she gets back, she'll have long-term therapy. The rape was only part of it, you know. He kept telling her what he'd done with Marsha. He even told her where Marsha's body was buried—in that little family graveyard behind where the house used to be."

Molly shuddered. "I guess she figured that's where she'd end up, too." She looked at Darcy and Scott. "Until you guys showed up," she added.

Tia lifted her soft drink in a toast. "Here's to you, Darcy. And your ESP."

Molly leaned forward, looking into the flames. "Mirror, mirror, on the wall," she intoned heavily. "Who's the weirdest one of all?"

"That's not a mirror, you nut," Kenny protested with a laugh. "It's a fire."

"Maybe," Molly said, staring into it, "but I'm seeing a picture anyway." She grinned at Darcy. "What do you think about that, huh?"

"I think you'd better blow out your marshmallow," Darcy said with a laugh. "It's on fire."

Hastily, Molly yanked it back and blew it out. "Seriously," she said, "without your ESP, Vickie might be—"

Tia shivered. "Seriously, I don't want to think about it," she said. "So what's the picture of?" she asked.

Molly leaned forward, staring intently at the fire. "It's a picture of an extra-giant super-size pizza with sausage, pepperoni, onions, and three kinds of cheese," she said. At that minute, the Masons's doorbell shrieked, with a scream that threatened to wake the dead.

"You heard the truck drive up outside," Darcy accused, sitting up and throwing a soft pillow at her.

"Did not," Molly countered with a laugh. "It was my ESP that did it."

Simon came to the family room door bearing a pizza in one hand and the ticket for it in the other. He bowed. "Your pizza has been delivered," he said in his deep voice. "Who among you, pray tell, plans to pay the delivery boy—" He held up the ticket and inspected it. "—fifteen dollars and thirty two cents, plus three dollars and twenty five cents delivery charge and a fifteen percent gratuity?"

"Since it was Molly's ESP that conjured it up," Darcy said, "maybe she can tell us how much that comes to."

Molly shook her head. "Sorry," she said. "My ESP just got cancelled out by my math anxiety."

"I'll take care of it," Scott volunteered, fishing money out of his pocket.

After the last of the pizza was eaten, Scott glanced at his watch. "Hey," he said, "it's later than I thought. I'd better get going. I'm on duty tonight."

"I'll walk you to the car," Darcy said, going for her jacket.

Outside, the air was crisp, with a clean smell, and the stars were bright. Darcy's breath was frosty as she walked beside

Scott to his car. "Thanks for coming over tonight," she said.

"Sure," Scott said. "It was nice." He leaned against the car and opened his coat and pulled her against him, wrapping it around both of them. They stood that way for a long moment, with his chin resting on the top of her head. She could feel his heart thudding against her cheek and his warmth soaking through her. *This is good,* she thought. *Quiet, sweet, and good—something I can count on, something I can trust.*

After a moment he tipped her head back. "I want you to know how proud I am of you, Darcy," he said quietly. "It wasn't easy, I know. But you hung in there, even when the rest of us didn't give you enough credit for—"

She put her finger on his lips. "Don't," she whispered. "I don't need any credit."

He chuckled and the corners of his eyes crinkled. "What do you need?" he asked.

Darcy raised her face toward his. "Just you," she said simply, and pulled his face down. His mouth was warm and gentle against hers. For Darcy, everything else faded into the dark night, and there were just the two of them, standing under the silent stars, together.